THE
PROGRESSIVE
REPORTS

A Manual for the Destruction of
American Values and Christian Morality

A Satire By

FRANK J. CONNOR

Post Hill
PRESS

A POST HILL PRESS BOOK
ISBN: 978-1-64293-339-0
ISBN (eBook): 978-1-64293-340-6

Post Hill Press
New York • Nashville
posthillpress.com

Published in the United States of America

For God, Country, and Family.

CONTENTS

PREFACE

History will record that we are in the midst of the most crucial battle our nation has faced since the Civil War. While no armies stand poised to attack our cities or kill our people, there is a force at work in our country that threatens to destroy, from within, everything we know ourselves to be. The war in which we are now engaged is for the soul of our nation, our people, and our values.

The social change that has been progressing for the past several decades is finally coming to a head. The morality on which Western civilization was built is now on the verge of defeat. The Church is rocked by scandal, leaving Catholics without a moral leader. The ancient civilizations of Europe have surrendered themselves to foreigners who seek their ruin. That once-proud continent has all but lost its identity. Our nation's founding principles are of little consequence to the majority of Americans, who are willing to sacrifice everything for comfort. We are in a vulnerable position, but we have it in our power to reverse our trajectory. We have it in our power to change the course of history by making the choice, always, to do what is right, even when it is difficult. Instead of being the generation that let the United States finally surrender the last vestiges of its values—letting it join the rest of the world in moral squalor—we can be the generation that puts our country back on the course that first led it to greatness. If we are to do this, we will need to understand the threats we face so that we might effectively combat them.

The correspondence enclosed in this book outlines some of those threats. They are a collection of several dispatches sent by progressive student, David Gore, to the Democratic National Committee. They outline his plan for the creation of a progressive future for America. It is unimportant how these documents came into my possession. Suffice to say, a friend of a friend entrusted me to bring them to the attention of the public. Because I was not their primary recipient, I am not able to date them precisely or place them in exact chronological order. I, therefore, ordered them myself, taking care to group together reports that were logically connected. In some places, I was, however, able to make educated guesses as to the order of these reports, but it is possible I am not privy to the entirety of Mr. Gore's mail.

It is also important to note that these are not necessarily the writings of an ideological zealot. They are the work of a man who seeks power for the progressive movement above all other considerations and are addressed to an organization more concerned with winning elections and gaining power than they are with any discernible principle. Many kind-hearted liberals, who are genuinely trying to do good by those around them, should justly find these reports offensive. They are as much victims of Gore and the Democratic National Committee as the conservatives the documents intend to undermine. My publishing what I have decided to call *The Progressive Reports* is not, then, intended to pit

Republicans against Democrats or conservatives against liberals. It is meant to shed light on the fight between what is
right and what is wrong.

Frank J. Connor
Villanova University
September 17th, 2018

INTRODUCTION

For the attention of the Democratic National Committee,

If the events transpiring at St. Augustine University of Philadelphia are any indication of things to come, the Democratic Party has cause for great concern. It seems the hold progressivism has had on the college population might be slipping at our school. I need not remind you how catastrophic it would be if conservative influence supplanted ours at the university level. But it appears to be the case. This university's chapter of College Republicans, under the leadership of a man we shall call "FJC," has announced its intention to fight back against all that progressivism holds dear.

In his club's introductory statement, FJC pledged his organization to be a platform for conservative students to express their vile ideology.[1] He pledges to create an environment where the "non-licensed non-conformist" can feel free to openly express his opinion without fear of social or—in some cases—institutional retribution. My fellow progressives at this university and I recognize how dangerous this can be. If it sets a precedent, this trend could sweep across the country and destroy, from within, the progressive society we seek

---

[1]   See Appendix A

to create, before it has the chance to take hold. We cannot allow this to happen.

It is for this reason that I have decided to pen a series of reports to you, the DNC, outlining the ways we, as a unified front, can ensure that conservatism is never allowed a chance to overwhelm the good intentions of progressive society. Over the weeks and months to follow, I intend to send the Committee a series of dispatches detailing my observations of conservative activities, as exemplified by FJC, and my recommendations for future actions, based on my experience facing conservatism daily at this university.

It is my most sincere hope that these reports will help the DNC bring about the destruction of conservatism and the antiquated values for which conservatives stand. If they had their way, the United States would be engaged in creating what Thomas Jefferson once called "The Empire of Liberty." Knowing the social, economic, and racial consequences this would have for the rest of the world, it must never be allowed to come to pass. To avoid this fate, let my words be an insight into the conservative mind. Let them inspire the Democratic Party to use its political might to change this country for the better. Let them serve the movement I love above all other things, guiding the United States to the progressive future it deserves.

David Gore
St. Augustine University of Philadelphia
February 27th, 2018

. 1:

Y POLITICS

In recent years, identity politics has become the cornerstone of our movement. Its importance in furthering progressive ideals cannot be underestimated. It is crucial in providing us the means of establishing a progressive future for this country. Identity politics allows progressivism to divide people into manageable identity groups, respectively addressing the key issues of our time: trans bathrooms, the wage gap, bigotry, and gender roles. The much-discussed economic and geopolitical issues are just distractions used by our conservative enemies to divert people from what is truly important.

Conservatives like FJC oppose our use of identity politics, chiefly because they are bigots, but also because they see it as a way to divide and distract the American people. This is complete nonsense, of course. Identity politics is a way to bring people together in the tribes with which they identify. FJC would say that such things only serve to destroy the national fabric of the United States, pitting these groups against one another and making us less of a nation. He fails to see the bigger picture. The emphasis he and conservatives put on treating everyone as an individual threatens social justice. It diverts our eyes away from the small groups we use to classify people. If we were to see everyone as an individual, how would we ever be able to determine which groups are oppressing each other? We would have to hold individuals responsible for their own actions instead of holding groups responsible for individuals' actions.

For the purposes of identity politics, personal identities can be divided into three main categories (though, of course, there are more): race, gender, and sexual orientation. It is important that progressive and all socially conscious people understand these aspects if they wish to utilize this strategy effectively. If used to its full potential, identity politics can help overcome the conservative ideology and the revolting American society for which conservatives stand.

Race

The advancement of progressivism requires that we always seek to boil down every aspect of a person or situation to identity. Race is usually easy to take advantage of, as it carries with it the most historical baggage and social anxiety. For this reason, every issue in society, every instance of conflict or confrontation, must be viewed as an issue of race. In every situation, the questions should always be asked: What was the race of the oppressor? And what was the race of the victim? (Every situation has an oppressed party, but straight white men are invulnerable to oppression).

The glorious Black Lives Matter movement has been extremely successful in this initiative. They constantly scour police dispatches across the country for instances of white police officers brutalizing defenseless young black men. They then masterfully cut through the irrelevant facts of each case to point out the truest cause of those acts of violence, the racial causes. By turning what would otherwise be just another overlooked instance of cold-blooded murder on the part of police into a national issue, Black Lives Matter generates a racial divide that further engrains racial identity into people's minds. Not only are they able to impress this difference in race into the minds of the affected minority group, but they generate this feeling within the oppressing group as well. When Black Lives Matter chooses to oppose acts of racism through peaceful protests—as have been seen in Fergusson Missouri and Baltimore where only $25 million in damages was done—they then expose racist white people in their midst. Anyone who questions the motives of Black Lives Matter or suggests that their protests should be suppressed because of a few completely justifiable acts of violence is clearly racist.

We should all follow the example set by Black Lives Matter. We should all look first at the racial parameters of the matter at hand without getting bogged down in the legal details or individual circumstances. Hyperawareness of race, then, is of paramount necessity. Once people become so aware of race that they are blind to the less important facts of a situation, it will be easy for us to make absolutely every act a racially motivated one. Race will be the cause of every-thing, and so any misfortune experienced will be seen to be not the fault of an individual, but an uncontrollable consequence of his race.

The implications of this are profound. Traditionally oppressed minority groups will be completely free of blame for everything that happens to them. When a black man goes to jail for murder he will be seen for who he truly is: a victim of the racist white system of justice. The dreamers, who come to this country by heroically running across an un-walled section of the border, are not breaking the law as conservatives heartlessly attest. They are simply defying a system that seeks to subjugate them and millions of other minorities. Whatever a member of a minority group does, then, is the direct result of their white oppressors and the inherent racism of those white oppressors.

The advantage to progressives of this racialization is that we are allowed to focus all of our attention on racial issues. We can completely avoid addressing the less relevant concerns of the majority of the American people. Hillary Clinton demonstrated this principle masterfully—it would have won her the election if not for Trump's treasonous Russian collusion. Clinton was able to cater to the social justice movement in her continuous battle against the character of Trump and his supporters. She justly labeled the majority of Americans "a basket of deplorables" when they opposed opening our borders to all who care to enter, when they dared to suggest that allowing millions of refugees from the Middle East into the United States might not be the wisest decision, and when they asked unreasonable questions regarding the reasons for poverty and crime among minority communities. Hillary was so successful because she swept aside the concerns of those "deplorables"—ignoring their existence altogether—and, instead, addressed racial concerns. Think of how poorly she would have done had she decided to travel to those dreary states in middle America to talk about the ways she was going to bring back their lost manufacturing jobs. Nobody really cares about manufacturing jobs. Nobody really cares about those people in the boonies between New York and California. Hillary was completely right to condemn them and their support for Donald Trump as the sheer act of bigotry it truly was. By writing these terrible people off, Clinton could appeal directly to the people oppressed by those out-of-work blue-collar workers and the social justice warriors in Brooklyn and San Francisco who really care.

This method allowed Hillary to avoid the pitfalls of taking a concrete position on policy initiatives to which conservatives tend to cling. Instead of asserting a position on US relations with Russia or presenting a platform on how she intended to deal with ISIS—assertions that conservatives would undoubtedly use against her if she failed to fulfill her promise—she doubled down on her emotional appeals. Consequently, she reinforced the beliefs of those who agree with her, while signaling to everyone who cares more about those geopolitical issues than race, that their votes are not wanted in *our* movement.

Hillary was able to gather millions of socially just supporters in this way while exerting minimal effort. By appealing to people's emotions and a genuine desire to make the world a better place for marginalized communities, Clinton was able to garner an almost religious level of support. For people dedicated to gaining racial justice, voting for Hillary was a moral obligation.

By using these techniques of social justice, the progressive movement can become the movement of racial justice. This exciting prospect would mean that, for the first time in history, America could see a truly dynamic political movement with the ability to dedicate itself entirely to racial issues and instances of racial unrest as they occur. This form of racial progressivism has the potential to exist outside the confines of the established political ideologies and can, therefore, apply emotional truths to every situation rather than rigid sets of principles.

The possibility for a movement stemming entirely from empathy is one that should inspire all caring people. Whenever injustice is inflicted upon a member of a minority community, the full force of progressivism should be turned to addressing that injustice and to making others face the injustice head-on. It is paramount in such cases that all of society stop to recognize the wrongdoings committed by some of its component members. Constantly working to resolve every individual issue in a mindful and progressive way will help us bring people into our movement by preserving a constant flame in the hearts of the caring. This flame will not fail to inspire the empathetic to adopt our movement as their own. What person with a heart and a desire not to be socially isolated would refuse to join a movement whose goal is to respond to acts of injustice committed against minorities? A person would have to be cruel and cold-blooded not to join our fight.

The college campus is the perfect environment in which to put this initiative into action. College students are always looking for an opportunity to be involved in something larger than themselves. This, coupled with a naturally active social conscience, makes them prime candidates to join a progressive movement that labels itself racially just. Here at St. Augustine, we witnessed the University Society for Racial Inclusion stage a march across campus in response to FJC's article placing more value on an individual's character than on his race. If words alone will draw enough energy in the college community to inspire a march, one can only imagine the level of dedication that could be mustered if these students were presented the opportunity to march against racist acts. It is also important to note that the dedication here marshaled can be diverted to other causes within the progressive movement that are not racial in nature.

Once we finally establish that our movement is the only one that promises racial equality, then every other group must, in the eyes of the public, necessarily be opposed to racial justice. Therefore, the conservative movement's opposition to progressivism—regardless of which aspect of progressivism they oppose—can be seen as racist. This incontrovertible fact gives us leverage that the conservative movement can never have. The advantage to us is that we never need to address the questions they raise. We can simply reinforce the notion that they raise the questions they do—and so render their responses—as a result of some deep-seated racial motive.

To elaborate on this point, it is useful to consider the recent example of Trump's travel ban—which was largely supported by Trumpists and conservatives alike. Most on the

Right would formulate an argument based on national security concerns and statistics. They usually argue that without a proper system of vetting in place, opening our borders to areas of the world that are known hotspots for terrorist activity—breeding grounds for terrorists—is unwise. They would say that Trump's freeze on accepting refugees from countries that are known exporters of terrorism is not only reasonable but the only sane option.

We know better. We know, first of all, that their motives are not born of concern for the American people and their safety, but born entirely of their bigoted hatred of the historically peaceful Islamic faith. Realizing that this is their only motive, we need not address safety concerns at all to win the argument. We need only throw accusations of racism at them. We are saved the inconvenience of wasting our time formulating concrete arguments addressing the concerns of our opponents. Again, the opportunity to increase the popularity of our movement is present in this method. In creating a single position for the opponents of conservatism to rally behind, individuals do not need to be well versed in any topic or argument to launch their own assaults on our political opponents. All they have to be able to do is reaffirm the line: those who disagree with the movement of racial justice are racists. Instead of a huge knowledge base being required—instead of needing to waste time thinking—a person on our side only has to be able to say the word "bigot," and our opponents are defeated.

While the conservative movement stands as a bastion of elitism, with followers who are required to be acquainted with such documents as the Constitution, progressivism is infinitely more inclusive. Instead of a person being forced to develop a set of beliefs on their own by absorbing information from the world around them, progressives are simply told what they should believe—making it easy to further the objectives of the movement.

The ultimate goal of progressivism's racial strategy has always been to create an environment where a person's race is the only factor in determining their political affiliation. By labeling our movement as the only one that defends minorities, we will be situated as the natural political choice for members of those minority groups. How could minorities fail to vote for the political movement that has their best interests at heart? We are the only movement that recognizes that their misfortunes are entirely the fault of white society.

While those on the Right think that minorities can be helped by a better economy and by providing them jobs and a means of escaping their situation on their own, we recognize that these poor people are incapable of escaping poverty on their own. We, therefore, believe that it is the responsibility of the government to provide them the means to live. Through progressive support for government welfare programs, we keep alive the impoverished minorities across our nation. By the grace of progressivism, minorities are able to survive.

For our tireless efforts, we are rewarded by minority groups with their political support. By convincing them that their salvation is in our hands alone, we have been able to make their politics a function of their race. We have proven ourselves so successful in helping the African-American community that 88 percent of black voters cast their ballots for Hillary Clinton in 2016. To a large extent, we have ingrained progressive politics into African-American culture, but we must go further.

We must seek a future where minorities cannot find a place for themselves anywhere but the progressive movement. This can be accomplished, partly, by continuing to convince them that Republicans and conservatives are actively oppressing them. Our popular culture does a great job of this. Popular music, such as rap, is riddled with accusations of brutality on the part of the police. The creators of this music are the few members of racially oppressed minorities who have taken advantage of the aspects of American life that allow talented individuals to become successful. They now use the fruits that the system has given them to subvert it and expose it for the cruel regime it is. By pointing out instances of police brutality—such as those identified by groups like Black Lives Matter—these musicians are reinforcing the belief that America is not safe for African Americans. It helps minorities realize what we progressives have been saying for over fifty years: that American society must be completely destroyed. Through his culture, we have convinced the black man that America is bad and requires progressivism to change the country in his favor. If we take action now to spread this knowledge to members of other minority groups, we can show them that they too require progressivism to solve their woes. We will be able to create a future where political ideology is inherited in the same manner as skin color.

Gender

While nothing is able to stir emotions quite like racial tension, its scope is too limited for it to be the sole vehicle for identity politics. It is therefore essential that identity politics not be limited to just racial concerns. To cover the ground that racial tension cannot, the leaders of progressivism have realized that they can tap into a minority group that makes up over half of the United States population: women. (I realize that it may sound incorrect to characterize women as a minority, but it is necessary that I do so in order to accurately display their lack of representation.) Identity would not be complete as a tool for the progressive movement without the addition of gender. Women and other non-male genders have taken the brunt of oppression by the majority since day one. We cannot pretend to stand for social justice if our movement does not also include them. Thanks to their vast numbers, these oppressed women have the potential to stand as the primary soldiers of progressivism. Many of them are from non-oppressed, wealthy white backgrounds, and have grown up surrounded by the privilege against which they now fight. They bring to the table resources that most racial minorities cannot.

While groups like Black Lives Matter fight against the racial oppression and the systemic racism confronting them, subjugated gender groups fight against the traditional Western gender roles and social norms imposed by white men. These norms act as socially constructed prisons—created by men to maintain their positions of authority. Women and members of other genders must hear and understand this point so that they understand what is truly happening to them (and so that they may be appropriately enraged by their social constraints). While far from being the most marginalized group in American society, women often face the brunt of male oppression. It is therefore important that we understand the struggles of American women and discover methods of alleviating their suffering, while simultaneously breaking apart the foundational elements of our nation.

Women in this country face discrimination of all kinds, but it is wage discrimination that affects them in a way most useful to progressivism. Wage discrimination is the name given to describe the average difference in the average man's salary from the average woman's. The United States Census Bureau has indicated that, in 2016, women earned only 82 percent of what men earned. Like with clear instances of racism, further analysis of this shocking statistic is unnecessary and unwanted, as it can only stand in the way of the more important narrative. Women are being discriminated against. Men are actively setting aside what is in their own everyday best interest by making the choice to pay women less than they deserve. If in this instance, we accept the conservatives' capitalist understanding of economics, we are led by this statistic to a very worrying conclusion. If the labor market is, in fact, competitive, and if companies pay higher wages to incentivize potential employees to work for them instead of their competitors, we must then accept that competitors are coordinating with each other to keep female wages low. If not for this huge discriminatory collaboration, companies would offer top dollar to hire the most qualified workers—man or woman—who could potentially make them the greatest profit. The level of coordination that goes into preventing every company in the country from exceeding the 82 percent wage limitation betrays the true extent of the efforts being taken to keep American women from achieving their truest potential.

Conservatives, apparently, do not see this mass discriminatory effort as a problem. Once again, as in the case with race, they turn a blind eye to the obvious injustice, paying no mind to the emotional state of the women this affects, instead turning to examine the heartless facts of the situation. They argue, as Christina Hoff Sommers does, that the 82 percent statistic is misleading and somewhat meaningless. They say that, as the mere measure of average totals in earnings between two genders, it does not take into account the differences in men and women's choices. It does not, for example, point out the fact that nine of the top ten most lucrative college majors are comprised overwhelmingly of men, while nine of the ten least lucrative college majors are comprised mainly of women.[2] Conservatives also like to prattle on about the amount of hours men work compared to women, the different life choices men make, and the differences in career paths—all of which, they say, whittles the wage gap down to a statistically insignificant percentage that can be explained—or perhaps mansplained—away by any number of things.

In arguing these points, conservatives, once again, demonstrate their inherent sexism. By suggesting that the problems being faced by women in this country are anything other than the fault of men, they insult the dignity of the female gender. They act as if a career path or a course of study is a choice for women, without realizing that every

---

[2] Sommers, Christina Hoff. "The Gender Wage Gap Myth." American Enterprise Institute. February 3, 2014. Accessed October 6, 2018. http://www.aei.org/publication/the-gender-wage-gap-myth/.

woman's choice is made for her by society. They act as if women are in control of their own lives.

It is important that progressivism continues to absolve women of the consequences of their actions, creating a culture where actions can be divorced from their negative implications. On the other hand, because all the forces acting against women are external, every time a woman is successful in any aspect, she should be viewed as a hero who has conquered a world acting against her. Embracing these characteristics of women in society has allowed us to build the image of the intrinsically heroic woman. By making it clear that women are always fighting oppression in their everyday lives, we can foster the notion that a woman must be extraordinary simply to make it through the day. They have to be tougher and stronger than men because they are fighting invisible forces that men do not fight—such as the gender wage gap. Fostering this new dynamic means progressivism can stand as the movement that puts women above men, the movement that claims retribution for women for a perceived history of men's wrongdoings. What woman would not want to join a movement that views her as virtuous based solely on the gender with which she was born (yet another uncontrollable aspect of her life)? This represents a complete departure from the traditional conservative values that sets men and women as equal and, instead, presents us a means of breaking down that conservative social structure.

It is the progressive understanding that traditional American society was created by white men to further themselves and subjugate those around them. To this end, they imposed rigid gender roles, which have become so engrained in our society that we feel as though we are born with them. For men, socially constructed gender roles dictate that they put effort into becoming tough, heroic, and able to stand up to any challenge, despite the odds. Our new assertion that women are intrinsically tough and, by nature of being women, already possess the attributes to which men aspire, undermines what it means to be a man. We have taken steps toward displacing men altogether and installing women in their stead. The progressive movement, then, offers women the opportunities men have always enjoyed, but in which women have never before taken part. In an attempt to destabilize American society in the 1960s, our forebears in progressivism taught women to covet the roles of men, but, today, we have finally created the means to deliver unto women the jobs and roles they were encouraged to desire. We have made it so that women can now be the men we told them they wanted to be.

When we first conferred upon women as intrinsic the virtues to which men have traditionally aspired, progressivism reaffirmed the true significance of those values. In doing so, we inadvertently reaffirmed the noble goals of traditional masculinity, making it necessary that women fight to attain that which men have always been taught to strive for. The obvious consequence of this is that, for women to live up to the masculine virtues laid before them by feminism, they must endeavor not to be content in their feminine characteristics, but to achieve masculine ones. A conservative might take from this the erroneous belief that the brand of feminism progressivism promotes is one that is setting women on a path to failure. By setting masculine goals before women and telling them to compete with men in being men, conservatives would say that feminism is leading women down a path to misery, not empowerment. They believe that a woman cannot possibly expect to be a better man than a man because it would be going against her nature. Further, they believe that it deprives women of the ability to achieve their fullest potential. The logic they use is that, by making the choice to pursue ends that are not in her nature, a woman would be departing from what makes her who she is. By departing from what makes her unique and by abandoning her skills in pursuit of a feminist goal, someone like FJC would argue that she has chosen not to fulfill her true potential, but to fail in achieving a potential that is not hers. This nonsensical argument is why conservatives tend to lean toward individualism and dislike our attempts to reduce people to their identity group. They want a world in which an individual, man or woman, can employ the full extent of their skills and abilities to achieve, for themselves, an end that is natural to them. While pursuing this ideology may result in some women embodying the masculine virtues of strength and toughness that feminists seek, it does not guarantee that all women will be viewed as strong and tough. While the individualist stance may, in fact, help women and improve their lives, it does very little to help the advance of progressivism.

Our movement depends on women fighting tooth and nail to be more like men because it generates friction between men and women. It is important that we make men feel as though women are trying to replace them in their societal roles. We have only begun this push, so it will take some time before the majority of men feel endangered, but, if we continue, we can create a fear within men that will lead them to push back against us and against feminism. This pushback creates evidence for us to show women that they are indeed being oppressed by men. By creating antagonism now, we are assuring the fulfillment of our own prophecy. We are ensuring that gender politics can remain a useful instrument of progressivism into the future. We can overturn these social structures not only by altering what it means to be a woman in modern America but by changing what it means to be a man.

It is no secret that traditional masculinity is the greatest problem affecting our society today. Men who act as gentlemen, men who serve their families as breadwinner, men who act with resolve and determination, are the men who most threaten the ascendance of social justice. The ranks of the conservative movement are comprised of these types of traditional men. Before we pose a solution to this toxic element within our society, let us first examine these "Alpha males" and determine exactly what leads them to stand in the way of the world we seek to create.

Everyone is familiar with this type of man. They have been the bane of liberal men's existence for generations. These problematic men are characterized by the ideals to which they tend to hold themselves. They place value on their physical, mental, and emotional strength. They have a high regard for courage, justice, and even such antiquated notions as honor. They are stubborn. The gentlemen among them value propriety, honesty, and modesty. The most dangerous—the conservatives in their midst—have an unwavering devotion to a set of core principles and the Christians to their God.

The value these men place on strength is troubling to a progressive movement that requires strong and assertive women. Strength in men is a natural threat to the further-ance of strong women—diminishing the joint efforts of progressivism and feminism. In physical terms, most men have a greater capacity to accumulate muscle mass than most women. A man that places value on exercise, sports, and accumulating muscle is bound to arrive at the point where he is outperforming his female counterpart due to his body's natural advantages. This contradicts the feminist position that men and women possess the same physical potential and capabilities. As we continuously see, biological assertions of difference between the genders is a common tool of sexism. It is therefore important that men are discouraged from gain-ing physical strength so that women may be given the oppor-tunity to achieve an equal level of physicality—furthering the feminist ideal.

Corporeal muscle is not the only type of strength valued by men that poses a threat to feminism and progressivism, the emotional fortitude in which the traditional American man prides himself is also problematic. One tends to think less of a man if he is not in total control of his emotions at all times. If he allows himself to be overcome by feelings of sadness or nervousness, he is thought to be less of a man. Women are, consequently, loaded down with the burden of emotional expression and, therefore, deprived of the emotional control used by men to overcome obstacles. For, as long as men hold this position of emotional strength, it will be very difficult to break through to them. The emotional appeals of progressivism—the foundational arguments of our movement—will have a much more difficult time getting a foothold in the minds of these men.

Perhaps the most dangerous aspect of the traditional American man is his propensity to fall victim to conservatism. The ranks of that movement are full of the stubborn men who value their principles above themselves. This type of man has a core set of beliefs, which are usually rooted in their faith in God and faith in their own purpose in life. He doesn't have opinions, he has convictions. He doesn't think, he knows. He knows that what is important is not himself, but God and his country.[3] This type of man subsequently does not serve himself—he does not enter politics in order to advance the cause of a particular identity group, as we progressives do—he seeks to serve his country and his God. To him, the hymn, *I Vow to Thee My Country*, is more than just patriotic propaganda, it is a promise.[4] Because he adheres to his principles as an act of devotion, he is always resolute and determined in his actions. These are the men who, in times of war, volunteer to put their lives on the line in service to their country and their values. Strong conservative men like FJC threaten progressivism because they do not bend. Their rigid defense of principle makes them invulnerable to the slow, but constant wearing down of American society that has always characterized the progressive movement. In

---

[3] With regards to a man's values, FJC would define a man's country not merely as a piece of land or a nation, but as the people who makeup that country. It is his friends, acquaintances, and the people around him. His neighbors.

[4] Lyrics in Appendix B

the arena of identity politics, their firm belief that an individual is responsible for himself alone stands in the way of our attempts to explode the will of an individual to the will of the identity group to which he belongs. Attempting to slowly convince him that the offensive language of white men, for example, should be suppressed in this country, as it has been in Scotland, is a futile effort.[5,6] The conservative man is not swayed by emotional appeals made to reject the right to free speech to save individuals' feelings, or so that an identity group can escape criticism. He pigheadedly sticks to his belief that freedom of speech is a God-given right and that one man's emotions cannot be allowed to dictate the innate liberties of another. There is no hope of defeating these individuals in open confrontation, they will invariably defeat us with principle and by force of will. The way we can best fight these conservative men is by outlasting them and by depriving them of a future. The key will be to not allow these types of men to develop in the first place. We must encourage virtues antithetical to conservatism and to traditional masculinity. We must breed a new type of man who will not stand athwart progressivism, social justice, and identity politics, as FJC and his band of conservatives do.

The archetype for this new type of man already exists in the millennial beta male. This spineless and unprincipled

---

5   Montgomery, Jack. "British Police Arrest At Least 3,395 People for 'Offensive' Online Comments in One Year." Breitbart. October 14, 2017. Accessed October 6, 2018. https://www.breitbart.com/london/2017/10/14/british-police-arrest-at-least-3395-people-for-offensive-online-comments-one-year/.

6   "Man Guilty of Hate Crime for Filming Pug's 'Nazi Salutes'." BBC News. March 20, 2018. Accessed October 6, 2018. https://www.bbc.com/news/uk-scotland-glasgow-west-43478925

creature of social fashion is exactly the doormat progressivism needs to advance the cause of social justice. This type of man is ideal because he is the sort of person that will not only fail to stand up for what is in his own best interest, but he will actively work against his best interest for the furtherance of progressivism and the feminist agenda. By his very nature, he smashes the gender roles his feminist friends so oppose.

The progressive man does not value strength. He is subservient. He naturally gives way to the women in his life, regardless of the issue at hand. He does this because he has an imbued sense that he is in the wrong, that he is responsible for all the ills that have afflicted women since the beginning of time. Instead of building up the women around him—as a conservative might recommend, to empower the women in *his* life—the progressive man lowers himself to give women advantages over him. It should be noted that, though it sounds virtuous, the conservatives attempt to elevate and encourage the women in their lives without lowering themselves is actually a terrible imposition on those women. It implies that women should have to do as much as their male counterparts in order to achieve the same level of success. If this were the case, it would follow that a woman is not owed anything for the sole reason of being a woman. This constitutes an undue emotional strain. The best way to strengthen the position of women in society is to weaken the position of their male competition.

In addition to smashing gender roles through their inherent weakness, progressive men diminish what it means to be a man by abandoning the social conventions of the traditionally valued gentleman. This is done in a number of ways. The first is a general abandonment of politeness and proper etiquette. A progressive man, for example, should never go out of his way to hold a door for a woman. He should, instead, treat women with the same level of disregard he treats his fellow man. When on a date, he should never take it upon himself to pay the entirety of the bill at a restaurant. He should always recommend some sort of division of the cost. When a man pays the bill at a restaurant, he is belittling women and taking self-respect and self-worth from them. In practice, this sharing of cost often becomes a necessity, as it is very important that progressive men encourage the women in their lives to be the breadwinners while they take a back seat.

This aspect goes along with the need for progressive men to lower themselves to provide an advantage for women. These men should not seek to find a job that can support them and their family; they should, instead, encourage their wives and girlfriends to pursue careers that support them. The millennial beta males on the cutting edge of our movement can again show us the way forward in this respect. They have shown us that one of the best ways to overturn American society, as it has existed, is for them to abandon ambition altogether. Where traditional conservative men hold dreams of achieving lofty aims and of being able to support their families, progressive men have had the clarity to realize how undesirable and difficult that can be. For this reason, they have chosen to set aside ambition for comfort. In college, many choose majors that do not challenge them and leave them ample time to pursue both their own pleasure and support the cause of social justice. Men who major in fields like

Gender and Women's studies have consigned themselves to a future where they are dependent on others for their wellbeing. They are then able to wage war against those traditional men who are arrogant enough to want to improve their own lives and take care of their family and the people they love.

It is important that progressive men undermine the culture of familial dependence on men. Being the core unit of American society, it is tantamount to the establishment of a new progressive society that the family dynamic be changed to assert women as the dominating role. Even though most of us know from experience that the woman, in most cases, appears to be the one making the majority of household decisions, the reality is that these women are entirely under their husbands' control and have no say of their own. Men must make up for this historic transgression by recusing themselves from their traditional role. They must renounce the position of breadwinner and seek always to put women in that desirable position. In doing this, they help America to create a progressive society by signing away their manhood as traditionally defined. Progressive men must embrace this new norm as a means of furthering the modern feminist ideals to which they ascribe—in many cases, more fervently than women.

It is their devotion to the modern feminist cause, that makes these men the noblest of creatures. They have forgone their own best interest to drive forward a movement that is at the forefront of the progressive cause. Because of their deep-seated sense of social guilt for the privilege they hold, these men are willing to do absolutely anything that appears to be in line with politically correct motives intended to right the wrongs of their forebears. They have only a vague sense of what exactly those wrongs are and would never dare challenge a woman's perception of those wrongs—meaning that they will do whatever they are told and fight for whatever value they are told is socially acceptable. Unlike conservatives, they do not question the principles behind the new initiative being pushed on them, they only look at who is giving the orders. If it is an individual claiming to speak for an oppressed minority group, they will immediately jump on board. This makes the progressive man useful in every aspect of the movement. Any time there is an argument needed to increase the size and power of the federal government—the historical goal of progressivism—the only thing we need do to rally mass support from these progressive men is to assign social justice motives to big-government goals.

These types of men are so easily manipulated because of their utter lack of rigid principles. While conservatives believe that stubborn adherence to their beliefs is one of their greatest strengths, we know otherwise. We know that the greatest principle of all is flexibility—in a sense, this means the total abandonment of principles. Conservatives like FJC take to heart Thomas Jefferson's quote, "In matters of style, swim with the current; in matters of principle, stand like a rock," but, because we know that virtually everything in our society is a social construct, we are aware that everything can be boiled down to style and social fashion. The progressive man operates on this assumption that the only important thing is the moment's social fashion. He, therefore, cannot stand like a rock on rigid principles but must be able to float with the prevailing current. He does this sure in the knowledge that he is doing the right thing. The implications of this are that a progressive man will, with religious zeal, carry out every protest and hold any position that is fashionable. This explains the swift explosion of belief in more than two genders and the number of people who defend this belief as if it is an eternal fact of humanity. By making it a popular concern and getting the right people to advocate for the reality of more than just two genders, these progressive men, who are so keen on advocating for those who they believe they have trodden upon, fill the streets at the first opportunity to advance the new cause. All we must do, then, is continue to popularize causes that are antithetical to traditional American society—like gun control—and we can bring millions of progressive men out of the woodwork, absolutely and unshakably convinced that their march to strip Americans of their fundamental rights is justified, that traditional America can become a thing of the past. By doing this, we can make virtuous—in the minds of millions of Americans—what is traditionally viewed as unvirtuous.

Abortion, for example, is viewed by those on the Right as a reprehensible and immoral sin. We, though, through our control of the popular culture, have completely altered popular perception. We have convinced millions that abortion, instead of being a sin which deprives an unborn child its right to life, is the most heroic expression of female independence. By relieving people of their ties to a rigid set of principles which leads them to make virtuous decisions, we can use popular culture to easily redefine what it means to be virtuous. We can replace institutions like the Catholic Church, which has guided Western morality for millennia, with reality television about dysfunctional and immoral families. Replace eternal truths with timely conveniences. Without the rigidity of principle required to put one's beliefs ahead of one's self, personal satisfaction can assume its place as the highest goal of humanity. The progressive man must fight back against conservative men who advocate ends higher than their own, who see their place in the world and their own importance as a very small part of a much larger picture.

Progressive men are overwhelmingly motivated to abandon traditional principles, not only to satisfy their own desires but to take on the title of "non-conformist." The non-conformist title is one that is valuable in its own right to the progressive man because it gives him a means of differentiating himself from the traditional American ideals of masculinity and of his societal function. The specific conformities that he opposes are entirely irrelevant in this respect. The virtue is not derived from that in which the progressive man believes, but from the fact that he does not believe what has been traditionally taught. It is for this reason that the millions of progressive men who oppose American society can rally together in a common non-conformity under a progressive banner to break apart that which conservatives value. In this way, progressivism stands as a totally unified front against all things traditional. On college campuses, we see the near hegemony of this non-conformist progressive ideology. FJC calls conservatives at St. Augustine "non-licensed non-conformists." He is quite clearly wrong. There is no non-conformism other than progressive non-conformism. The progressive movement requires the value placed on, and the uniformity in, this non-conformity to incentivize men to overcome principle and bring the restructure of masculinity to its logical conclusion.

In the end, masculinity has to be altered, as to accommodate entirely the culture of identity politics and social justice that is pushed by the progressive movement. Men will assume a far more diminished role in our society to make up for their history of transgressions against women. To do this, men will increasingly be portrayed in popular culture as idiots, inferior to their female counterparts. Progress has already been made in pursuit of this goal. One only has to watch a comedy on television to observe as the man is almost always a lovable fool who is constantly trying to hide his mistakes from his quick-witted wife. Gone are the days, thank God, of knowledgeable and principled male characters like Ward Cleaver and the television dads of a half-century ago inciting young men and boys to adopt traditional masculine principles—the sort often held by conservative men today. A progressive future is one in which male characters are derided and encourage young men to avoid principle in favor of personal pleasure and satisfaction. They must encourage the creation of a population of progressive men who actively combat their own advancement, lowering themselves so that women may all rise above them—achieving just retribution.

Men's outward-facing devotions must accordingly be to the people who their distant ancestors have historically oppressed. They must take on the cause of social justice to make up for those past transgressions and submit to the guilt of their identity. Men must assume, as a whole, the responsibility of those individuals in their midst who do wrong toward women. Should the progressive male become the norm in America, every man will feel the guilt and shame that goes along with one man using his male privilege to surpass a female. Every man will be indicted for every instance of abuse against women. Punishment and censure will be diffused throughout the male population, undermining any moral claim that a man might make and leading to a situation where the only defensible positions men will be allowed will be positions of unquestioning support for the groups they oppress.

Progressive men will, therefore, be entirely obedient to the progressive movement, making them the perfect tools for spreading the movement and destroying the society it stands against. Progressivism will have an army of people ready to follow the social fashions we push forward and fight for our message because we have taught them that they may have none of their own. They will religiously promulgate the messages we create about social justice, identity politics, and topics which are discussed elsewhere in this document, because not to do so would be an act of apostasy for men to whom progressivism is divine. As a result, we will never be without people to push our message and vote for our candidates when they run for office. The soul of America will be irreversibly changed by progressive men who wish to destroy the nation that, in less than 250 years, rose from violent birth on the outskirts of civilization to the greatest force for good—as the conservatives would say—that the world has ever seen. The men who fired the first shots at Lexington and Concord, the men who fought for the Union at Gettysburg, and the men who stormed the beaches of Normandy and Iwo Jima are dead—their values and principles consigned to history.

In their place, we have soldiers of progressivism, sworn to destroy the society created by men of the past.

Where possible, it is ideal to go beyond changing what it means to be a man, and, instead, discourage a man from being a man at all. Alternative genders are, therefore, a major part of the progressivist future of America. Once the social constructs—which have confined the free expression of the American people—have been eliminated, as they are being eliminated, the development of non-traditional genders can go into full swing. Already, we have created a culture in which it is considered virtuous to allow young children to make free choices about their imbued nature. We have a significant portion of the population that has so recognized the irreparable harm done by the traditional gender roles that have been socially imposed on us since the dawn of human existence, that they are willing to take the noble step of encouraging their children to turn away from the usual path. Parents who see even mild effeminate behavior in their son for what it truly is: a cry to break away from systemic societal oppression—these parents are enlightened enough to realize, even before their children's brains have finished developing, that their kids have been born with the brain of another sex. More than acting out of supreme enlightenment and irreproachable tolerance, these parents are acting in support of progressivism. These parents are on the front line in the war for identity politics. They are physically creating new identities that will be marginalized by traditional society and therefore require the support of progressivism.

Just as we want race to dictate political leaning, we want gender identity to do likewise. It is already the case that the majority of individuals who identify as a gender other than male or female are progressive in political persuasion. We can, therefore, expect support for our cause to grow as we increase the number of people who choose not to identify by one of the two traditionally accepted sexes. To encourage this alternative identification, it is important that we make being other than male or female a virtue in and of itself as we have begun to do with women. This case, though, differs from women in that it challenges societal norms by the nature of its very existence. For this reason, it is a natural generator of antagonism. Many on the religious Right will oppose efforts to encourage alternate genders, seeing it as going against the nature of the individual. These people are just standing in the way of progress. They may cite tens of thousands of years of evidence that there are but two "real" genders, but we know that, here, in the United States in 2019, we have succeeded in discovering this crucial fact about humanity that history's greatest minds had not.

With this sureness of purpose, we go forward to spread gender non-conformity and widen the umbrella of progressivist protection. For our sake, the future must be one in which the social fabric of America is destroyed by the fragmentation of its constituent members into minorities banded together for the sole purpose of staging a social *coup d'état.* This will spell the end of FJC's beliefs. His movement will be asphyxiated by our depriving it of the very people from whom it is composed. A nation with an indefinite number of genders will never listen to a man who espouses notions of traditional morality rooted in Catholic faith. Such people will not accept that a nation should be governed by principles when they can be governed by the social fashion that is the reason for the very existence of their genders.

Sexual Orientation

FJC's note in our university newspaper quite curiously fails to mention sexual orientation in its tirade against identity politics. For this reason, I think, before we go into too much detail about the ways in which our movement can exploit non-traditional sexual orientations, we should try to piece together exactly what it is that FJC and his conservatives believe. To do this, we will have to make inferences based on his constitutionalist, conservative, libertarian, and Roman Catholic background—God forbid we just ask him.

Examining his libertarian leanings, which are evident from the emphasis he places on freedom and liberty in his introductory statement, the conclusion that we tend to reach is that FJC does not care all that much what two individuals do in their own home. This is the general libertarian sentiment on the matter of homosexuality: the belief that there are no grounds for external authorities to involve themselves in actions between two consenting adults when no external harm is being inflicted. The freedom of choice—which may, according to FJC's theology, differ from true freedom— is engrained in our American psyche and vanquishes any impulse FJC might have to suggest the forcible cessation of homosexual practices. This may present a hairline fracture in his Catholicism.

His libertarian beliefs would, accordingly, also extend to his stance on gay marriage. Libertarians want very limited government interaction in individuals' social lives, as there is no imperative for the government to act where one individual does not require protection from another. This would lead a libertarian-minded conservative, like FJC, to the conclusion that government has no role to play in marriage, whatsoever. As far as the law is concerned, any union of any two people would be admissible under a simple bilateral contract. This is, after all, how marriages used to be legally established. For those only interested in being united under civil authority, FJC must see this arrangement as more than sufficient. Insofar as marriage goes beyond civil union, the libertarian in FJC likely believes that one's religion is the governing authority in marital affairs.

The constitutional argument would extend itself from this religious point for FJC. The First Amendment to the US Constitution guarantees freedom of religion and that government shall not adopt an established religion. Government intervention in the practice of a religious ceremony, such as a marriage, is therefore constitutionally prohibited. The caveats to this occur when the religious practice endangers the wellbeing of society or of a participant of the practice who is incapable of representing his or herself for whatever reason— examples would include underage marriage, incestuous marriage, any kind of forced marriage, and so on. Given this line of logic, FJC is forced to accept that gay marriage cannot be legally prohibited insofar as it takes place as a religious ceremony. Logically, then, if a homosexual couple found a church and a religion willing to marry them, there would be nothing to stand in their way, legally.

Above, we have outlined the beliefs FJC holds about the legality of homosexuality, but, as a man of devout Catholic faith, we should also attempt to understand his moral opinion on homosexuality. For this, we should bring our attention to the Catechism of the Roman Catholic Church—to FJC, the authority on all matters of faith and morality. To my understanding, the Catechism informs Catholics that "everyone, man and woman, should acknowledge and accept his sexual identity."[7] In the cases of homosexuality, it instructs individuals to abstain from marriage and sexual relations, as they cannot take part in the objective of creating human life. The Church also affirms that, through chastity, faith, and the practice of Catholic life, homosexual Catholics may achieve "Christian perfection" in the same manner as heterosexual Catholics.[8]

If FJC has any personal beliefs or opinions that diverge from the accepted Catholic teaching, they would most likely center around the strictly asserted purpose of sexual relations and marriage. He might say that, in its ability to serve as an expression of love and commitment, a sexual relationship might be admissible beyond procreation—this is probably just his feeble attempt to escape the confines of his faith and justify sin. This minor flexibility might theoretically, however, justify the existence of homosexual relationships and

---

[7]   Catholic Church. Catechism of the Catholic Church: Revised in Accordance with the Official Latin Text Promulgated by Pope John Paul II.Vatican City: Libreria EditriceVaticana, 1997, 2333. http://www.vatican.va/archive/ccc_css/archive/catechism/p3s2c2a6.htm

[8]   Catechism of the Catholic Church, 2nd ed., 2357-2359. http://www.vatican.va/archive/ccc_css/archive/catechism/p3s2c2a6.htm

allow homosexuals to escape undue suffering for an uncontrollable aspect of themselves.

Despite his possible personal beliefs, as a Catholic, FJC must, as a matter of faith, accept the ruling of the Church as absolute. We can, therefore, paint him as entirely against the social movement we stand behind and use the conservative unwillingness to cave to us, as a means of the creating friction and turmoil, which act as a catalyst to the progressive movement.

The only way we can really make the existence of alternative sexual orientations work for us is by painting them as oppressed by the traditional American majority. We must smother the notion that there are people in this world who agree with FJC—whose position is logically derived—or worse, that the majority of people, perhaps, do not care about the issue of sexual orientation at all. We need non-heterosexuals to need us. If we cannot present ourselves as their only means to salvation, we cannot count on their support in every other aspect of our movement.

In order to do this, we need to focus on two main goals. The first is bringing sexuality to the forefront of popular thought—most people do not spend very much time thinking about the sexual orientation of others unless they are directly confronted with it. The second is to paint opponents of progressivism as opponents of non-heterosexuals by nature of their very existence. This sets us as the sole defenders of the LGTBQ+ world while also immediately barring non-heterosexuals from hearing the truth about what men like FJC believe.[9]

---

[9] LGTBQ+ stands for "Lesbian Gay Transgender Bisexual Queer et al."

By proclaiming the virtue of pride in one's alternative sexuality, we have driven the LGTBQ+ community to flaunt their sexuality at every possible opportunity. We have created a country characterized by gay pride parades and television shows meant to glorify homosexuality as an ideal far superior in virtue to heterosexuality. We have already achieved the mass popularization we needed it to achieve. Thanks to our success, an overwhelming number of homosexuals now "acknowledge and accept" their sexuality—surely, FJC would rejoice in this fact. We have reached a point where there are few people in this country who do not know a member of the LGTBQ+ community, and so there are few people who feel comfortable taking a position that stands in the way of their advancement. This first victory paves, for us, a road to the next requirement of our movement, one on which we have already made great progress, alienation of the LGTBQ+ community from conservatism.

To do this, we must simply continue spreading the message that the Republican Party and people on the political Right hate homosexuals. We have to beat this into the popular consciousness at every possible opportunity. Constancy is crucial because the main evidence we have to support this claim is the popularity of the claim itself. There is little to no concrete evidence of Republican politicians taking actual actions to restrict the rights of LGTBQ+ people in recent years. To placate the few who do demand concrete evidence and in order to create news cycles forwarding this message, we must rely on an exaggeration of individual acts and statements to levy our accusations on the whole of the political Right. Soundbites from fringe Republican candidates in minor elections, out-of-context remarks from Republicans on Capitol Hill, and selective historical citations provide ample evidence.

With this picture painted of conservatives, we have significantly diminished the likelihood that a member of the LGTBQ+ community would even dream of investigating the validity of any movement other than progressivism. By severely dissuading exploration of alternative ideologies, we have all but trapped members of the non-heterosexual community within the confines of our movement. We have cut them off from alternative messaging and placed them in an echo chamber of our design. We can then batter them with our ideology and our accusations against conservatism and traditional American society, sure in the knowledge that conservatism will not leak in.

The purpose of our echo chamber must be to incite severe hostility and aggression against conservatism and conservative values. Our messages must encourage rage and inspire marches to take place against traditional America. We need to make the LGTBQ+ community believe that they are fighting for their lives against a group of people, not unlike the Nazis. We must make them feel as though they have been backed into a corner by society while keeping them ignorant of the fact that most of society has never given their sexuality a second thought. When we are finally able to assert complete control over non-heterosexuals' attitude and emotions toward the world, we will have them in our pockets, they will be creatures of progressivism. LGTBQ+ will be synonymous with the progressive movement.

Once the term "gay Republican" becomes an unfathomable concept to people on both sides of the political aisle—as will be the fate of the terms "black Republican" and "female Republican"—we will have finally brought identity politics to its logical end. We will have created a culture in this country where a person's political identity and ideological beliefs are dictated entirely by the unchangeable characteristics with which they were born. Being black will make you a progressive. Being a woman will make you a progressive. Being gay will make you a progressive. The United States will be so socially engineered that belief will be prescribed at birth. In this way, we will become less of the destructive form of humanity which has existed on this Earth for millions of years, governed by thought and reason, and we will go back to our roots and be governed by a new sort of socially constructed instinct. If we get our way, our politics will gain total control over your identity.

REPORT NO. 2:

WHY WE MUST FIGHT RELIGION

Unfortunately for the progressive movement, there exists, in this country of ours, a persistent belief in God. This belief has permeated the national soul of the United States since the country's inception. In our Declaration of Independence "we are endowed by *our Creator* with certain inalienable rights," President Washington petitioned God for His help upon first being sworn into office—a tradition which continues to this day—and our national motto is "In God We Trust." No wonder, then, that God and religion play such a major role in the lives and politics of our adversaries. William F. Buckley Jr, the patron saint of the conservative movement was, like FJC, a devout Roman Catholic. President Reagan, the hero of the right wing, was the first Republican politician to truly embrace American evangelical

Christians. The political Right is filled to the brim with men of God and men of faith. If we wish to defeat the conservative movement, we must undermine the entire nature of religion in this country. We must deprive traditional America of the foundation of their way of life. We must create a country with a new set of foundational beliefs that lead people away from conservative values and into the light of progressivism.

Before we can institute our new form of progressive religion, it is important that we have a clear understanding of what we are up against. We must understand the beliefs held by the conservative movement. We can do this by analyzing FJC, the man who has come to represent conservatism at our university.

When taking on FJC, we are taking on a man who prays his daily rosary in Latin. This is a man for whom his Catholic faith is at the center of all he does. We can assume that Christianity plays an equally important role in guiding his fellow conservatives. This role affects, primarily, the conservative process of decision-making. The core dogmas of their faith provide them a set of very clear and strict principles that they must apply to everything they believe. These strict principles center around the core moral imperatives of the Catholic Church—affirmations about human dignity, charity, compassion, and love. In his introductory statement for St. Augustine College Republicans published in *The Hippo*, FJC applied his faith by claiming a desire to "[push] back against the pervasive trend of moral relativism" when he stated that "[his] values and morals are rooted in the core dogmas of the Church and in the word of God, making them eternal and absolute." The brand of moral absolutism that FJC advocates would return our country to a time when right and wrong were not dictated by social fashion and when compassion did not equate to the blind tolerance we now preach, but was much closer to its Latin derivative which means "to suffer with." A country beholden to these Judeo-Christian values is not one which we can long tolerate. It is antithetical to our way of life and, ultimately, destructive to society as a whole. The past two thousand years of the Church's existence have been characterized by nothing but oppression. We must bring the world back to the way it was before the advent of the Christian morality these conservatives claim has been the driving force in the success of Western civilization for two millennia.

Along with instilling rigid morals in individuals—morals that make the advance of progressivism a laborious one—the belief in God sets a hierarchy where something other than the immediate desires of humanity is of supreme importance. It encourages a belief in a power far above government and beyond the control of progressivism. To destroy this unhelpful hierarchy, our movement must include a rejection of God as one of its goals.

It is because of the dangers presented to our movement by the Christian beliefs stated above—because of their belief in absolute morality, in God, in Christ as our savior, in the Holy Trinity, and in the doctrines of the Catholic Church—that we must fight against religion in general and Catholicism in particular. Conservatives' faith undermines the goals of our movement, and so our movement must strive to undermine every aspect of their faith. In order to do this, we must fight to encourage moral relativism, we must encourage atheism, we must establish government as our only savior, and we must turn faith in science into the new and infallible American religion.

Moral Relativism: Why We Need It

Though moral relativism is not a familiar phrase to most members of our movement, its creeping progression has been the driving force behind some of our greatest achievements. Few realize that, without the persistent crawl of relativism, progressivism would never have achieved such victories as abortion on demand, something most of us today take for granted. Like mold on a piece of bread or termites in a tree, moral relativism slowly but surely eats away at the foundations of American society without any upheaval and often without any warning signs. While Christians believe Christ will save them and lead them to Heaven, we believe the quiet onslaught of moral relativism will deliver us the pleasures of Heaven on Earth. Moral relativism is more essential to the function of the progressive world that any Christian delusion about God could possibly be.

At the center of moral relativism is the understanding that there should be no objective standards in our society, but rather a floating set of standards dictated by the popular social fashion of the moment. We have, over the years, taken steps to remove these objective standards from our culture. Through the use of media and television, we have been able to alter the moral criteria by which people are judged. Instead of deferring to their religious institutions for instruction on right and wrong, the American people increasingly turn to television, movies, and pop-culture icons. Television programming constantly sends messages encouraging people to do what makes them feel good about themselves and to do only what makes them happy. In a departure from the miserable family programming of decades past, which invariably culminated in some corny moral lesson rooted in traditional American and Christian beliefs, programs today are above such lowly assaults shaming people into positive behavior. As a result, we have begun to create a society where people's morality is not based on the lessons they learned in Sunday School, or on the bible, or on the teachings of the Church; their morality is dictated to them by what they see every day. It is dictated by what *we* put in front of them. We have told them that right and wrong are not real, that everything is some shade of grey and, therefore, there is no wrong moral answer. We have told them that they shouldn't compare themselves to anyone or anything. We have told them that they alone have the means of determining what is good and bad because, ultimately, it is only their personal happiness that matters.

We can push these beliefs that were, for centuries, understood to be wrong because people want more than anything for them to be right. Nobody wants to do what makes himself unhappy. Nobody wants to have to apply strict rules to himself and the people he loves. The easiest way for us to make people choose to do wrong is to tell them that what they want to do, is the right thing for them to do. These constant affirmations of individuals' feelings and impulses allows us to degrade adherence to the rules Christianity places on us all. Cardinal Ratzinger, in his homily opening the conclave that would see him elected Pope Benedict XVI, stated precisely why our movement must embrace relativism and move away from Church teachings saying,

> *"Today, having a clear faith based on the Creed of the Church is often labeled as fundamentalism. Whereas relativism, that is, letting oneself be 'tossed here and there, carried about by every wind of doctrine,' seems the only attitude that can cope with the modern times. We are building a dictatorship of relativism that does not recognize anything as definitive and whose ultimate goal consists solely of one's own ego and desires."*[10]

Though, in this statement, Ratzinger is condemning our relativist aims—saying later in the homily that we progressives are like children being "tossed about by the waves"—he does do a very good job of defining it. Our movement is born of the desires of the individual, as he claims. It is the only ideology that can match the constantly evolving desires of humanity. To double down on two-thousand-year-old beliefs simply because they are the word of God, the creator of Heaven and Earth, is idiotic. Who can seriously suggest that the objective standards to which men and women compared themselves in the year 33 AD should be the same as today? Perhaps the best instance of this we can consider is that of abortion. The teaching of the Church is unequivo-

---

[10] Cardinal Joseph Ratzinger, *Mass: Pro Eligendo Romano Pontifice,* Vatican Website, April 18, 2005. http://www.vatican.va/gpII/documents/homily-pro-eligendo-pontifice_20050418_en.html

cal—and obsolete—on this matter. Pope Saint John Paul II stated in *Evangelium Vitae:*

> *"that direct abortion, that is, abortion willed as an end or as a means, always constitutes a grave moral disorder, since it is the deliberate killing of an innocent human being. This doctrine is based upon the natural law and upon the written word of God, is transmitted by the Church's tradition and taught by the ordinary and universal magisterium. No circumstance, no purpose, no law whatsoever can ever make licit an act which is intrinsically illicit since it is contrary to the law of God which is written in every human heart, knowable by reason itself, and proclaimed by the Church."*[11]

The hard laws on abortion dictated by the Church are simply not a fit for our modern times or for the goals of our progressive movement. As I stated in the section on women, far from being a grave moral disorder, abortion is the highest expression of women's liberation and freedom. To take the life of an unborn child should be seen by all as women finally overcoming the limitations put on them by our contemporary American society. Our relativist push on abortion is so pervasive that even many on the political Right fall victim to it.

Because of our work, many who claim to be realistic pro-lifers are doing much of the legwork in making the

---

[11]   Pope St. John Paul II, *Evangelium Vitae*, Vatican Website, sec. 62, 25 March, 1995. http://w2.vatican.va/content/john-paul-ii/en/encyclicals/documents/hf_jp-ii_enc_25031995_evangelium-vitae.html

relativist position wholly pervasive. This brand of pro-lifers often accepts the need for abortions in the first trimester, for various reasons. They accept the establishment of a timeline over which the validity of life inside the womb changes. In a way, they have demonstrated a level of morality far further from Christian teaching than have progressives who believe in abortion up until the very last minute. While most progressives believe that the fetus is not a human life until birth, which makes it admissible to end the pregnancy prior to birth, conservatives who do not mind the practice of first-trimester abortions do accept that life begins at conception. They are the ones who are condoning murder. They do this because they have been fooled by our ability to make grey a black-and-white choice. We have changed the argument from one of life and death to one of pain and suffering. We have convinced these people that it is okay to terminate the life inside the womb, so long as the pain incurred by the unborn is negligible. FJC described this as "a morality not based on true right and wrong, but one based on a compromise as to the level of wrong allowed to take place."[12] This is a perfect example of our ability to remove objectivity from consideration of good and evil.

In abortion, we have ensured that there is no fixed standard to which men and women must hold themselves. We have destroyed the dichotomy of good and evil, instead insisting that evil might not be so bad after all. In doing this, we appeal to the baser instincts of humanity. The drive within people to indulge themselves. By eliminating the need for

---

[12]   Connor, Frank J. "Returning to Moral Absolutes." Western Free Press. October 22, 2017. http://westernfreepress.com/moral-absolutism-frank-connor/.

one to hold oneself to what is objectively good, we give him license to pursue whatever evils he desires.

This process is a slow crawl. In the case of abortion, first, we had to convince people that first-trimester abortions are really not that bad, as the fetus is not able to feel anything at that stage. Once abortion became allowed on a small scale, it wasn't a huge step to push the issue. If we're allowed to terminate a pregnancy in the first trimester, it is merely a silly deprivation of women's rights not to allow them to end it in the third trimester. Once the license is initially granted, our friend, the slippery slope, takes over and it's all downhill from there.

Through this tactic, we have the moral flexibility to appeal to people's desires. While Christians have always to look back at the bible and the Church for knowledge of their morality, we can make moral what people want to be moral. We can control morality. For Christians, that is a power reserved for God alone, for progressives, it is one we hold in the palm of our hands. We have the power to tell people that what they are doing is right.

We have the power to liberate people from responsibility for their actions, to effectively absolve them of their sins—a privilege usually reserved for God, through His Church—by virtue of rendering their sins naught. In doing this, we have established a society where those of a progressive persuasion are free of the moral boundaries established by institutions like the Catholic Church. The liberal may guiltlessly follow the moral guidelines established by the progressive move-ment. In this, they get a sort of freedom that Catholics can never attain.

The Church states "there is no true freedom except in the service of what is good and just. The choice to disobey and do evil is an abuse of freedom and leads to the slavery of sin."[13] The freedom defined by the Church is not the sort of freedom that people want. People want total freedom of choice. The ability to do whatever they want without having to worry about moral implications, without having to worry about what anyone else wants—including God. Progressivism can not only offer people freedom of choice, but it can offer them freedom from God. It can offer them freedom from the constraints of His Church.

The world is in dire need of this sort of liberation. It is no secret that, for the past two thousand years, the Church has been doing people serious harm. Today, it destroys the lives of women by not letting them destroy the lives of the unborn. Its teachings on divorce, adultery, and promiscuity stand athwart the inclinations of modern society upon which our movement depends. The Church is constantly warning people to concern themselves not with now, but with eternity and the future of their souls. But we know better. We know that life is meant to be lived here and now, that the freedom our movement provides, allows us to exploit, to the fullest extent, all that we are capable of doing. It is our seventy or so years on Earth that are truly important, not the eternity of the afterlife. It is then vitally important that we focus not on such notions as "grace," but on Earthly pleasures. We should not focus on the state of our souls, but on those fleeting physical sensations that enhance the experiences of the body. Sex, money, and drugs should be constantly in our minds.

---

[13]   Catechism of the Catholic Church, 2nd ed., 1731-1738.

The social conventions on sex have evolved continuously in our favor. With every social movement comes another cry for sexual liberation. Though this was taken to its height in the 1960s and '70s, it remains a helpful result of relativism to this day. Because of the progress we made a half-century ago, it is now the case that the first consideration for most men in contemporary American society is sexual in nature. Instead of taking into consideration God, family, and country, our movement has ensured that the baser instincts of man prevail. In doing this, we are able to distract from larger issues. As long as people's minds are distracted by their own sexual needs, we can carry on the business of expanding government and encroaching on the personal lives of the American people. Also, by encouraging people to seek out these Earthly pleasures above all other considerations, we can reinforce the notion that, through progressivism, humans can create Heaven on Earth. We can further steer them away from God and away from considerations of the afterlife as we encourage them to satisfy themselves in this life. In this way, through the grind of moral relativism, our progressive movement can begin to deliver now the promises made by God for life after the mortification of the flesh.

Money, like sex, has always been one of the driving motivations in man that best replaces heavenly aspirations. While monetary wealth in those who stand against our movement should be admonished—as a means of detracting and weakening their argument—the accumulation of wealth by those with whom we agree should be glorified. The actors, producers, and directors of Hollywood, who overwhelmingly support our ideals, should be held in the highest esteem and their earnings should be envied. We must create an obsession with wealth. Wealth may be either envied or demonized, but it must always be talked about. The obsession with wealth creates a drive in people that can entirely replace theological motivations and considerations. The pursuit of money must always replace the pursuit of Heaven because money is far more flexible. A man whose sole motive is the accumulation of wealth can justify even the greatest sins, likewise, a man whose sole motive is the redistribution of wealth can be driven to acts of cruelty on levels not seen since Stalin's purges and persecution of the Kulaks.

Relativism allows us to make some forms of wealth more acceptable than others. Because there are no objective grounds for assessing the morality of wealth, we can create whatever moral grounds we like. We can convince the American people, through media and political rhetoric, that the wealth acquired on Wall Street is evil, while the wealth generated by Hollywood actors and reality television stars is enviable. In this, we turn the tables. We demonize those bankers on Wall Street who are responsible for investing in new technologies and businesses which create jobs for millions of people and improve the lives of everyone in this country. These people are not inherently progressive. They are driven not by social justice motives, but by the desire to make life better for themselves and their families. Conversely, the wasteful extravagances of our Hollywood idols are highly moral. Instead of using their money to create more working people and more potential conservative voters, the "Real Housewives" of this world spend their money in ways that add to their own personal image and inspire younger generations to mimic them.

They, therefore, do not feed the endless cycle of economic growth which produces conservative voters and bolsters the harmful traditional American society. Their wealth is good wealth. Wealth made on investments is evil. By creating this dichotomy and glorifying the wasteful wealth of Hollywood, we encourage people to be extravagant in their everyday lives. We encourage them to spend money on what makes them feel good. To use their money to generate pleasure for themselves instead of to enrich others—after all, it is the government's job to take care of others. A focus on money—not God—can, in this way, bring one to a state of heavenly bliss.

Even with the accumulation of money and the sexual pleasures that lead one to experience the Heaven on Earth that progressivism promises, everyday human suffering still tends to leak into people's lives. To escape this worldly suffering, progressivism, once again, comes equipped with the best possible solution: drugs. While the Catholic FJC would tell us that this life is not what is truly important and that the suffering we endure here on Earth serves a higher purpose, we know that this is not the case. We know that suffering should not just be borne, but rather stifled. We have at our disposal a wide array of narcotics which allow us to make our time on Earth into our own personal paradise. While conservatives carry their crosses and take on whatever suffering they must to protect and preserve the racist country they love, we can escape to an altered state of reality—one of pleasure and enlightenment. Our forefathers, the progressives of the 1960s and '70s, knew full well the power mind-altering narcotics can have. They knew it as a means of disconnecting from the world around them and embracing their own form of reality—one free of suffering and consequence. This new reality was one where the "hippies"—as the conservatives of the day labeled them—could experience true enlightenment within their own minds. They realized that they had the means to achieve paradise within themselves and, therefore, did not have to be concerned with the good and evil preached by the Church. They had their own personal spirituality which was unassailable and free.

This is what we as progressives have to get back to. This is what we are fighting for. We need to restore the "religion of the self" back to our society. The personal and Godless spirituality of the 1960s and 1970s is one that sets free members of our movement, allowing them to fulfill themselves and bring themselves to an unparalleled Earthly happiness. To do this, we need relativism. We need the abandonment of objective standards of good and evil which stand in the way of personal happiness and progress. We need a new freedom—the freedom of choice not bound to the objective good of God. It is by these means that we entice followers to our movement. Without moral relativism, there is no future for progressivism.

Atheism: Why It's a Good Thing

Before progressivism can take its rightful place at the center of the lives of the American people, it is necessary that we eradicate the belief in God currently gripping most of our countrymen. The hearts and minds of the American people cannot be truly ours as long as we permit them to devote themselves to Him.

In return for living a life in the grace of God, in death, a Catholic is promised the eternity of Heaven. In Heaven, these Catholics experience the glory of God, they see God and exist in perfect communion with Him, the source of all that is good. By its very definition, there can be nothing better than Heaven. It "is the ultimate end and fulfillment of the deepest human longings, the state of supreme, definitive happiness."[14] Progressivism cannot compete with that. We need for the American people to be satisfied with those things we can promise them. We need them to seek no more than can be delivered by government and by progressive social programs. We need to defeat God in order to keep people looking down—in order to keep them in their place. (The place we made for them.) The American people should not be illumined by God but enlightened by progressivism.

Progressivism is a movement on the cutting edge of social thought and science—especially gender science and environmentalism. It is a byword for enlightenment. As such, we are able to proclaim all that we preach as the pinnacle of human understanding. Concepts such as destiny—which have inspired great men from George Washington to Winston Churchill—can be utterly dispensed with as old and obsolete.

FJC believes that:

> *"Destiny, most simply put, is what happens when one makes choices that further God's plan. As an example, for Winston Churchill, it transpired that*

---

[14]   Catechism of the Catholic Church, 2nd ed., 1023-1029 http://www.vatican.va/archive/ENG0015/__P2M.HTM.

the choices he made throughout the course of his life, which he knew to be right, led to outcomes which prepared him for, and placed him in, the situation for which he alone was qualified—being Prime Minister in 1940. When we strive to do what we know in our hearts to be right—in matters great or small—we move ourselves closer to the future that God most wants for us. The future for which we were born. The pursuit of destiny under God is one of man's highest pursuits, for it means continuously doing one's part to carry out His ultimate plan—acting as a utensil of God's will."

The elimination of destiny is, therefore, important as it deprives an individual of any hope of personal greatness or glory in this grand plan, leaving him nothing to strive for. Without a concept of destiny, of having a role to play in the history of the world—in God's plan for humanity—there is no longer cause for dreams. Man is left without goals to fulfill, without self-assurance, and without purpose. For progressivism, it is necessary that we are able to remove from the lives of Americans the natural sense of purpose imparted by a faith in God. For the purposes of our movement, life must not be what God makes it, but what *we* make it. Allowing men to dream of achieving their own goals and letting them live in the pursuit of their own destiny, is not conducive to the culture we must foster. We cannot tolerate a nation of Winston Churchills. They are simply too difficult to handle. The future and purpose of every individual must be sublimated to the future of progressivism. It must be realized by all that there is no future outside of the progressive movement.

Deprived of a God-given destiny and with progressivism as the driving force in society, it will not take the American people long to feel as though they require progressivism to do anything noteworthy. Alexis de Tocqueville recognized that: "despairing of resolving by himself the hardest problems of the destiny of man, he ignobly submits to think no more about them. Such a condition cannot but enervate the soul, relax the springs of the will and prepare a people for servitude."[15] The American people will need our movement if they wish to make something of themselves. Men of ambition, then, will have no alternative but to seek a home in the progressive movement or risk being overshadowed by it in history. For this reason, progressivism will have complete control of a country free of God.

With total loyalty to, devotion to, and focus on progressivism, we can finally reject the Judeo-Christian teachings which have endured for the last several thousand years. We can move beyond that static hierarchy that places God at the top and us at the bottom. We can free ourselves of the bonds of God's ancient laws. Christ's imperative to "love thy neighbor as thyself" can be disregarded.

When we no longer have to hold ourselves to loving our neighbors, we become free to hate—free to undermine, slander, disregard, and let suffer. We will gain the freedom to hate those with whom we disagree. In the past it was true that one could disagree with someone's political opinion, but, because of the insufferable confines of Christian social ethics, one had to respect that differing opinion. One was forced to have

---

[15]   Alexis de Tocqueville and Henry Reeve, *Democracy in America*, A Bantam Classic (New York: Bantam Books, 2000), 531.

some regard for the wellbeing of the man, even if his opinion was a conservative one. Free of Christ and his command that we love one another, we need not care about the wellbeing of a person who espouses such hateful beliefs.

We can, therefore, instruct the members of our movement to commit acts of violence against these horrible people if we so choose. We can, at the very least, arouse such feelings of hatred and disgust that anytime a conservative opens his mouth, he is instantly attacked by our loyal hoards. Such occurrences are prevalent on college campuses around the country. When conservative speakers, like Ben Shapiro, dare show their face at schools like the University of California Berkeley, violent protests erupt in response. This is just the type of hatred that we need to build in the country as a whole.[16] This hatred will motivate progressives, it will move them to momentarily overcome their pusillanimous natures and take action to degrade and destroy their conservative opponents. Our movement is nourished by the energy that only pure hatred can inspire.

This is completely at odds with everything Christianity teaches. At its foundation, Christianity is a rejection of the hatred we need to inspire. Christianity is built on love. As St. Augustine reminds us, "God is love." If this is the case, God is incompatible with the tactics of our movement. If this is the case, a Christian would be forced not to hate his political

---

[16] One has the scene from George Orwell's *1984* in mind where Winston Smith and his coworkers are brought into a room facing a television and shown images of Emmanuel Goldstein, the principle enemy of the state. Upon seeing this man's face, the room erupts with hatred and rage. The office workers were so taught to hate this man, that otherwise normal people are brought to the point of throwing chairs at the television.

opponent, but to love him, because anything less would be a rejection of God. For this reason, it is important that we conflate the love Augustine had in mind, when he made this statement, with the sort of lust which can briefly make a man happy. Augustine was not talking about love as the romantic Valentine's day fare we often view it as today. He was referring to a love born of general care and concern for a person. To love someone, in this context, is to want what's best for her and to want her to accomplish that which God intends—and to help her do so when possible. If love, as a concept is to exist at all, we need it to be in a form that does not contradict hate. We need it to be purely lustful. There should be no consideration of anyone but one's self and one's own pleasure. This love, born of animal instinct, is one that is void of God and, therefore, subject primarily to hate. By encouraging an abandonment of love by changing its definition in this way, we are able to isolate people from one another on a spiritual level. They will not be able to feel love for one another beyond the purely physical sense, because they will not have God in their lives to be the source of the truest form of love.

By abandoning God, we free ourselves from the conformity of religion. Our movement can become the sole bastion of hope for the advancement of the individual. In claiming to free him, we will subjugate him to our will—to the common good of all. By rejecting God, we reject the imperatives of love, which stifle our movement, allowing progressives to attack their conservative opponents with the visceral hatred required to defeat them. With hatred to push us forward, we will not falter. We will hate conservatives and the God they claim to serve. The future of progressivism is atheist. The future of progressive America is a nation where people tolerate each other insofar as their best interests are served, but where dissent and disagreement are met with unparalleled resentment. If successful, what we see today on college campuses like UC Berkeley, the growing level of racial animosity, and Christianity's decline among millennials portends our future.

Government as our Savior

To whom does a nation bereft of God look for its salvation? Government.

Once free from the constant and all-knowing eye of God watching our every movement and showing us right from wrong, the American people will need to turn to another entity for guidance. The American people will be forced to turn to the government. Without the shadow of God looming over the United States, the government will reign as the supreme Earthly authority. Without religion guiding the American people, the federal government will become the institution that tells people how they should live. And, while we have not yet gained the strength to control God, control of the government is never far out of reach of the progressive movement.

Humans crave an authority figure. They crave someone or something to emulate. Traditionally, in this country, it has been the role of the nation's religious institutions to provide such guidance. John Adams said of the United States, "our constitution was made for a moral and religious people. It is wholly inadequate to the government of any other." In saying this, John Adams speaks to the dependence the American people have always had on God. It was unimaginable, at the time of our country's founding, that people would rely on their government as a source of personal or moral guidance. It was engrained in our culture that government was a mere tool for achieving harmony in society. A tool which must constantly be wielded by a moral people.

It is good, then, that the government of the United States has, in recent years, grown to a size that allows it to appear as the strong authority figure our people can look up to. The United States government *is* power. There is no other force in the history of civilization whose power so overwhelmed the Earth. The whole of the free world is under the protection of the United States military. There is no entity this side of Heaven with a comparable level of force. Only God has the capacity to affect his will more decisively and more violently than the United States. It is only natural, then, that the American people, who cannot so clearly see God, look primarily to the United States government as the supreme being. After all, a government that can—at the touch of a button—bring all life on Earth to an end must also have the power to deliver to humanity all it desires. Once the American people see their government possessing the powers of God, it is only a small step for them to start assigning to it the characteristics of God—to start demanding from it that which only God can promise.

The government, under President Obama, also started taking steps to further insert itself into the lives of the people. The Affordable Care Act set the United States on the road to universal healthcare—the ultimate goal being a system on the

European model. In this action, the former president began to assert the federal government's position at the center of the individual's life. By having control over a man's healthcare, he has control over his life. We have seen this in the case of Alfie Evans, a two-year-old child in the United Kingdom who was removed from life support and allowed to die against the will of his parents because the National Health Service made the decision that his life was no longer worth the time and expense of the British government. In this case, the boy died because the government withdrew its will to let him live. This is exactly the sort of authority we need the United States government to possess. We need it to be in total control of every aspect of the individual's life. We need it to have absolute power over life and death. As the movement that has historically most supported and most taken advantage of government, giving the government power means giving progressivism power. If government has the power of God, the power of God will be in progressive hands.

With the power of God, we will be able to sweep aside conservatism entirely. With the might of the United States government behind us, we can begin to provide for the American people in a way that God does not. Progressivism will be the movement which saves the people from poverty, starvation, homelessness, and their every illness. We can provide them with a truly utopic society and bring to them *now* what Christianity tells them they must wait for. Conservatives promise freedom and the opportunity for an individual to realize his full potential. They seek only to provide for the soul with no regard for the body. They are purely aspirational, while we are the people who are in touch with reality. We know the concerns of the people. We know that they are far less concerned with the fate of their souls than they are with the fate of their material selves. For that reason, traditional religion cannot satisfy them. Never did God promise free healthcare. We do. By our grace and good nature, the federal government can be employed to create Heaven on Earth.

Because of government's ability to deliver what God does not. Because it has the power and might to provide for the basic needs of humanity—what is truly important—government should be praised as God. It should be served as God is served. Our lives should be lived in devotion to it—for it is progressivism.

"Ask what you can do for your country." The words of John F. Kennedy should ring in all of our ears as we seek to serve our new God. One of the most obvious ways to serve the country or, more specifically, its government is through the annual sacrifice we make when we pay our taxes. Taxes represent our commitment to our government, our support of its doings, and our continuing faith in its ability to serve us. We do not, currently, pay what we ought to pay in taxes. The amount of taxes that the American people pay today is enough to sustain, but not to further grow government. It is an amount of money that shows that the American people are only willing to tolerate government as long it delivers to them that which was originally expected of it. Taxes in a progressive world will show our profound appreciation for all that the government can do. Taxes should, therefore, liberate the people of the vast majority of their earnings. Why not? Government is, after all, the highest power. The omnipotent progressive government we seek provides for all the material needs of man. It would be selfish for an individual to keep too much of his income. It would be selfish for him to want more than just that which he physically needs. A man should not try to achieve anything aspirational while another man cannot. There is no room for individualistic behavior that degrades the position of the state in the lives of the American people. No man shall put himself before our new savior. And no man should believe that he can make for himself a better life than government can make for him. It must be the continued belief of our people that government can deliver all that a man could ever desire. If the occasion arises where government is unable to provide for the needs or wants of its people, it must be the job of the progressive movement to tell the people that what they are being greedy and unreasonable. The capitalist pigs who build mansions instead of paying their fair share in taxes and living like the rest of us should be condemned for their selfish indulgences. These people cannot be allowed to use their earnings to surpass the rest of society. They would be putting on display a level of opulence and personal prosperity that cannot be secured through our public institutions. The rich should not be able to display a behavior that undermines America's belief in the notion that government could bring to them all the happiness they desire.

FJC's personal hero, William F. Buckley Jr., described the situation we so desire in an interview, saying, "I think it's happening because of a restlessness. For so long as liberalism suggested it could bring happiness to the individual, then people tended to look to government agencies for those narcotic substitutes [in] a search for happiness and contentment which they ought to have found in their religion, in their institutions, in their culture, and in themselves." The fact is that the progressive movement must always strive to act as a replacement for the institutions Buckley speaks of in this quote. Progressivism has to replace things like religion and American culture if it is going to be as all-encompassing as we need it to be. Since progressivism is the natural friend to big government, we must make it apparent to the American people that the government can fulfill the promises made by religion. We must use the government's power and position in American society to make it into a God-like figure. It should, if things go right, replace God in the minds of Americans. With this in place, the progressive movement will become to government what Catholicism is to Christ. Our movement will become the only vehicle for delivering salvation to the American people.

Science and Religion

Government is a great replacement for God in the lives of the American people. However, it is tangible and, therefore, does not serve as a perfect enough substitute for the Christian faith in the eyes of the people. To truly replace religion in the United States, we must look to something more intangible, more mysterious, and more ritualistic. We must look to science. While moronic Trump supporters look to God for salvation, we are smart enough to realize that we can put our faith in science to save us from the greatest dangers in the world. While conservatives and Catholics seem to believe that science is responsible, primarily, for determining how things happen, we know that it can give us a definitive answer as to why everything occurs. This makes it the perfect replacement for religion in our society. It is one which is far more concerned with the human situation on Earth than any religion ever has been. While religion looks to God and to life everlasting, science looks to our immediate and tangible surroundings.

One might not, at first, understand why we need to replace religion at all. One might ask why we cannot just do away with it and live free from the constraints of any sort of guiding light. The answer is simple and has very much to do with human nature. Humans need an explanation as to why everything happens the way it does. If we were to simply disestablish Christianity in American society, people would turn to other means of personal enlightenment. These other means might not be ours to control. I will discuss the means of shifting the American people's faith from religious institutions to science in another report, but one principle that must be understood is that progressivism requires Americans to reject the teachings of Christ regarding the nature of the world in favor of the ones we present. We have to get them to accept that science is not the means of understanding *how* the world works, but *why* the world works. For this reason, we must induce them to believe that there are some people in the United States today who have the answers to the nature of the universe, while also believing that the Son of God does not. In doing this, we will create a nation of men and women without firm religious guidance and governed by the changing landscape of science.

De Tocqueville says, on this point, "When the religion of a people is destroyed, doubt gets hold of the highest portions of the intellect, and half paralyzes all the rest of its powers. Every man accustoms himself to entertain none but confused and changing notions on the subjects most interesting to his fellow-creatures and himself."[17] By replacing religion with something directed by humans, such as science, we can create a state of confusion for as long as people seek enlightenment. With citations from a myriad of scientific reports—which very few Americans understand—backing our claims, we can claim whatever we would like. The progressive movement need only back its emotional appeals with quotes from small segments of scientific findings to change the social landscape. We can make our laws—our edicts—with the gravity of the scientific community behind us. It is unimportant if science actually backs our position in full because we need to toss the American people scraps of the truth in order to confuse them and push through our agenda. They are paralyzed and are unable to defend themselves from us. Without the religious foundations on which to build their convictions, we are easily able to persuade the people to accept our initiatives with carefully edited versions of science.

Void of religion, the draw of science provides people an immediate focus for their attention that cannot be found elsewhere. It is concerned with our immediate needs, without regard for any form of salvation in death. It is, therefore, natural why so many would flock to it for unfaltering guidance.

A great example of this comes from the world of psychology. The notion that, through science, we can determine aspects of the human soul is a valuable method of controlling the population—the progressive movement has

---

[17]   Tocqueville and Reeve, *Democracy in America*, 531.

not yet exploited this as it should. Psychological personality testing—which has become widely utilized in corporate America—is a way of inserting science into an arena that used to be controlled by religion in order to deliver immediate satisfaction and comfort to the individual. In the past, personality was seen as a function of the soul. A person was not what some grid of personality types told him he was; a person was defined by his or her God-given nature and potential. The movement of the atheistic scientific community on which we rely has been away from such things as God-given nature and human potential when assessing the person. Through personality testing, psychologists have been able to reduce people simply to their temperament and the way they react in certain situations. They then fit them neatly into a personality type with other people who have corresponding reactions and temperaments. In doing this, the individual is stripped of his individuality and everything that makes him unique. He has been analyzed by means of some scientific method and been given a place in the world. Instead of going through the arduous task of determining one's vocation in life—what Christians believe to be one's God-given purpose—we have simply provided the individual with a group of people with whom he can identify using our own—human-centric—method. These pre-determined personality types often come with a list of jobs for which the person being tested might find himself suitable. Despite the disagreement within the psychological community about the validity of these tests—many psychiatrists would refer to it as mere pop-psychiatry—it remains a more scientific means of discovering an individual's nature than religion. It is, therefore, another progressivist affirmation that what matters is not God's plan, but temporal concerns.

Any major emphasis on science alone will reinforce the fact that this world is all that is important. Environmental science allows us to create something not very far from a worship of the planet itself. Along with using science to learn more about legitimate concerns about the more legitimate global temperature concerns, progressivism has used it to craft solutions to the problem so that they might increase their level of control over the American people. Progressivism starts by increasing rhetoric to its own members about the impact modern American society is having on the environment. Once these ideas make their way through the ranks of the Left, our members will walk away with the words: "the American people are destroying the Earth" bouncing around in their heads. It then goes into the collective responsibility we all have for the Earth that has provided us so much. The response of the young idealists within our movement is to set themselves in a position where it is up to them to defend the planet from everything assailing it. In a very short amount of time, the situation becomes one in which environmentally conscious progressives begin to elevate the Earth to a position in their lives, which their Christian counterparts reserve for God alone. They begin to worship the Earth because it is the logical conclusion of the tidbits of scientific environmental findings we have fed them. They then religiously demand an increase in the size and powers of government to curtail those practices which we have defined as detrimental to the Earth, giving us the perfect pretense to enact laws we have been pushing. This process of using an engrained belief in science—one held, in some capacity, by the vast majority of Americans on both the political Left and Right—demonstrates the political potential of cementing an absolute devotion to scientific conclusions.

As soon as such devotion is established, the American people will begin to believe that humanity is capable of understanding all things on its own. People will believe that there is nothing outside of human comprehension and that the secrets of the universe and the meaning of our existence are all to be found by scientific means. If our survival can be secured and assured through scientific means, why should there be any reason to believe that our existence cannot also be explained by scientific means? Progressivism can imbue, in the American consciousness, the notion that we can understand the reasoning behind all things—the "why" of all things—completely independently of a knowledge of God. With this abandonment of God in the consideration of all things comes the logical belief that everything which exists now, ever has existed, and ever will exist, is a product of the natural world. With this fact at the center of human understanding, the only conclusion that can possibly be reached is that we humans are limited to the confines of our natural Earthly existence. From there, the principles of moral relativism begin to take hold, leading progressives to abandon the objective right and wrong of God and instead focus on what makes men and women happy. The progressive movement will, at that point, be left to focus on doing that at which it is best, providing Earthly satisfactions to placate the American people, while conservatives continue to offer only a means to elevate the soul.

REPORT NO. 3:

HOW WE FIGHT RELIGION

The reasons for fighting against religion in the United States should be abundantly clear. Religion fundamentally stands in the way of everything the progressive movement seeks to accomplish. It prevents the sliding moral scale we so desperately need and occupies a place in society which should be reserved for our movement alone. For these reasons and for all the reasons stated in my last dispatch, this report will outline ways the progressive movement can, and should, combat religion.

How to Fight Moral Absolutism

Defeating the moral absolutism espoused by FJC is not a difficult task. It relies only on convincing the American people to do what is easy instead of what is right. That they should concern themselves with their own pleasures above all else. That they should treat all thoughts, ideas, and emotions as equal to each other. That they should not strive to be compassionate, but rather try always to be tolerant of other people—with the obvious exception of conservatives—and their eccentricities, regardless of what those eccentricities might be.

In one of his typically abhorrent articles on moral absolutism, FJC writes about the distinction between compassion and tolerance:

> *"Being better individuals requires us to recognize our faults and even to point out the faults in others. The problem is that many people today conflate compassion and blind tolerance. We are often told that it is compassionate to let people do as they please—especially when it runs contrary to what our society has always taught was right. It is, apparently, compassionate to allow children to alter their biological sex, but questioning a person's poor life choices makes one uncaring. This attitude completely rebrands compassion as a form of blind tolerance where the objective is not to help a person, but to avoid making him feel bad.*
>
> *The word compassion comes from the Latin word "compati" which means to "suffer with." Compassion should then be viewed as co-suffering. A compassionate person is not one who allows another to give in to the temptation to do evil. A compassionate person is one who assumes respon-*

sibility for another and helps him make the right decisions."[18]

As FJC suggests, we have already begun to degrade the practice of compassion by promoting the far easier practice of tolerance. People, in general, are instinctively lazy. Any time they are given an excuse not to do what they see as difficult, they will take it. It is very difficult for people to act with true compassion. Compassion is a genuine imposition on a person's life—an imposition that Christ instructed his followers to bear—it requires individuals to go beyond themselves and serve others. It requires the individual to love those around him—to want others to succeed in God's plan for them— which requires the individual's love of God to be possible. Tolerance, on the other hand, is not quite so difficult.

The blind tolerance we need to instill in the psyche of the American people plays on the laziness of every human. We must encourage the population of this country to believe that it is a far better thing to allow people to do what they would like than it is to tell them what is right. That the moral thing to do is not to try to help lift people out of their poor behavior but to look the other way and allow that behavior to take place because it is "none of your business." The American people should keep to themselves and worry about their own pleasures, rather than involving themselves in the lives of others. If parents would like to allow their child to alter his biological sex, they should be allowed to do so. It does not affect my life or yours, so it should be allowed to take place without our interference. We should simply write these things off as everyone being unique and different. We should encourage

---

18   Connor, Frank J., 2017.

them to do what makes them happy, because, ultimately, to us, there is no higher aspiration than personal happiness and pleasure. Instead of being so condescending as to force our own morality, or the morality of the Church, on another person, we should encourage every decision they make. His immediate happiness—not his future or his soul—is what is truly important.

This form of blind tolerance is born not out of love, as compassion is, but out of laziness, which makes it an easy sell to millennials, who are used to things coming easy. To be tolerant, one must only focus one's attention inward, which is natural in humans and comparatively effortless. It also requires no effort or interaction with the object of this tolerance. Where having compassion requires one to take on the pains being suffered by another and working with him to improve his situation, having tolerance requires one to sit back and do nothing. It requires a person to be idle as his fellow man does wrong or moves away from achieving his full potential. Once people enable others to do wrong, it becomes very easy to blur the lines between right and wrong, potentially eliminating that line altogether.

It should be understood that good and evil are relative terms. A thing can only be good when it has the bad to be compared to. In this good and evil are social constructs, just like gender. It has been the constant oppression of thousands of years of societal constraints that created these now-outdated labels. Everyone living in the 21st century should realize that our knowledge and our capacity for thought far outweighs the generations of teachings on the nature of good and evil. We now know that good and evil are subjective.

They are determined by the practices of the cultures defining them and the age in which they are being practiced. The stoning to death of rape victims in Somalia and slavery in early America are prime examples of the moral subjectivity determined by time and place.[19]

With this new understanding of the nature of good and evil, the American people will begin to abandon the concepts altogether. They will see that, because of the subjectivity of the words, they mean nothing. It will become clear to anyone who dares concern himself with the issue that there is no such thing as good and evil, right, and wrong, or even morality. People will come to the conclusion that only the emotional wellbeing and the general happiness of the individual are important—these, of course, will be divorced from any traditional moral considerations. With morality, as we now know it, defeated, humans will be free to do whatever pleases them. They will be free from the guilt imposed on them by their religious institutions and empowered to do what suits them, with little concern for others.

When discussing the need for moral relativism, I looked at the example of abortion as an area in which the progressive movement's push for moral relativism has succeeded and serves our cause. The effort to encourage women to abort their children is also one which further perpetuates moral relativism. Every time an abortion takes place, the value of human life, in general, is degraded in American society.

---

[19] Chesler, Phyllis. "Punished For Being Raped and Accusing Rapists: Women's Burden Under Sharia." Breitbart. October 28, 2014. Accessed October 6, 2018. https://www.breitbart.com/national-security/2014/10/28/pun ished-for-being-raped-the-burden-of-women-under-sharia/.

Every time a child is killed so that the mother's life may not be adversely affected, the lines between good and evil are blurred in the eyes of the people and every other narcissistic practice which damages the lives of others for the purposes of avoiding responsibility is encouraged. For this reason, abortions must continue.

To have this practice continue, and to gain support for it, the American people must be told that it is a means of empowering women. It should be seen as a necessity for the advancement of females and one of the paramount aspects of maintaining a woman's health. In doing this, we need to convince the people that death is life. We need to have them beg for death because they believe it encourages a happy life. "Give me abortion or give me death" should be the cry of every feminist in the United States. We must blind those who would call themselves Christian to the fact that only Our Father Below is served by the deaths of millions of unborn children. With the universal permission of abortion will come a new sexual revolution which will further bury the traditional morality of our society in its own pleasure.

By removing all consequences from sex, the progressive movement can present a clear reason to the American people why traditional morality is outdated. The elimination of the possibility of having a child—a prospect which frightens most unwed people—means that sex will be able to become as banal a recreational activity as going to the beach. With the prospect of a child removed from the equation, the Church's assertion that sex is for the purposes of procreation will fall flat, as most people will, by then, have created a clear distinction between the two in their minds.

They will view the Church's teachings on this issue as more of the same old outdated preaching that may have mattered to people living in the ancient world or in the middle ages, but which is completely irrelevant for people living in the 21st century. The result of an erosion of any portion of faith is dire to the Church. Once we have made it possible to question one aspect of the faith and properly ridicule it as out of touch with the new norm we are creating, the door is open to question more and more pieces of Church doctrine, eventually rejecting the institution as a whole—removing all objective morals from our society.

Along with this subjectivity comes an equality which helps inflate relativism. It is not an equality of opportunity, like the one promoted by the conservative movement. It is not a level playing field where laws do not disproportionately favor one group over another. It is an equality of sameness. Good and bad are not really different, but two sides of the same coin. Qualitative aspects are unimportant, and society is purely democratic.

With the aforementioned destruction of the objectivity of good and evil comes a belief that positive and negative are just two different perspectives. This is not a difficult position to argue. Love and hate are perhaps the best emotions to demonstrate this principle. The amount of emotional energy expended on love and hate is usually about equal. While we know that, as St. Augustine said, "love is God" and hate is a rejection of God, it is not hard to convince someone who knows no better that they are really the same. We need only say that feelings are feelings and it matters little which of them one has. We need to blur the lines between love and hate in this way so as to strip love of its objective meaning.[20] To do this, the progressive movement should take advantage of the false conflation of love and lust which we have long encouraged. By convincing people that lust and love are the same, while simultaneously associating hate with lust—think of all the movies where characters, in a fit of rage, go to bed together—we can fool people into thinking that love and hate are not opposed to one another. We can teach people that hatred is healthy—when directed toward our political enemies. This will not only wean people onto relativism by breaking down objective distinctions, but it will also eventually lead to loneliness in individuals as they seek only lust—failing to create meaningful connections with one another. The push to remove the distinction between positives and negatives like love and hate is also a failure to distinguish concepts on a qualitative level.

By removing the ability of the American people to make qualitative assessments on the issues we are pushing at the moment, they will, for example, be unable to see the difference between socialist welfare policies and private charities in taking care of the poor. They will not be able to distinguish between abortions and mammograms in the discussion of women's health. They will not even be able to tell the

---

[20] "The modern approach to love is essentially subjective: it is preoccupied with the subject who loves and with his psychological and moral dispositions. The Thomistic approach is essentially objective, since a power is defined by its act and its object: it is preoccupied in the first place with the object of love—namely, the good... The value of love is derived from the dignity of the object loved and not directly from the dispositions of the loving subject."—(Bonino, Serge-Thomas. Angels and Demons: A Catholic Introduction. Thomistic Ressourcement Series, volume 6. Washington, D.C: Catholic University of America Press, 2016.)

difference between a person telling a joke and a person being serious, because, to them, there will be no distinction to be made. Language will be language; women's health will be women's health; welfare will be welfare and, regardless of circumstance, it will all be created equal.

The progressive movement has always used this tactic to some extent, but never with the totality available in this new world of social justice. In the past, we were able to remove the qualitative differences between the United States and the Soviet Union—as it suited us—by labeling them both as aggressive empires while failing to acknowledge what each was fighting for. Many on the Left viewed the United States' actions in Vietnam in this light. Because of our painting of a geopolitical stage where the mighty United States was pushing around the poor farmers of Vietnam, we were able to skirt reality and condemn the United States government as an imperialist power. Instead of it being plain that the communist forces of North Vietnam sought to subjugate the free peoples of the South and claim the country for communism, progressives were able to alter the narrative to make it seem as if the Vietnamese people were simply attempting to change the nature of their own government—and would have done so peacefully, but for the intervention of the United States. While this narrative could not be farther from the truth, in the late 1960s and early 1970s, this total breakdown in qualitative differentiation allowed the progressive movement to mobilize millions of young idealists against the United States and established American institutions. The anti-war movement produced by this principle was where the progressive movement adopted the sort of rhetoric and imagery we use today.

A huge aspect of the progressive movement during the Vietnam War was the demand for a more democratic society. It was those brave young people on the streets of Berkeley who began to demand that our progressive voices be heard; that everyone is deserving of representation and equal treatment. For our movement to succeed today, and to secure a relativist future, it is important that we pursue these demands as promises to the American people.

We need to show the American people that progressivism is the only option for those who dislike the hierarchies of institutions like the Catholic Church. The Church, as a whole, is antithetical to the democratic values of our progressive society. First of all, the notion that one must go out of one's way in the service of God is incredibly insulting. Why should any person have to wake up an hour early on Sunday to worship God? The notion of worship, in and of itself, implies that one thing is inherently higher than another in the celestial order. Democratic principles, however, tell us that we are all equal and that we must all be treated equally. Worship of God, therefore, is undemocratic. Then the whole hierarchy of the Church—priest, bishop, archbishop, cardinal, pope—is out of step with the modern world and with modern distributions of power. In pursuit of our rejection of the absolute standards of behavior imposed by the Church, the progressive movement must present itself as the alternative to the Catholic hierarchy. It must present itself as the only rational belief system for a person who refuses to bow to any power—even God—because of the value he places on his own independence and on the pride he takes in his status as equal to all that surrounds him. The same democratization of society, which promises the progressive that he will always be equal to those around him, also suggests that all religions are equal and all ideologies should be viewed equally—except for conservatism.

To defeat Christianity and the objective ideals for which it stands, one of the tactics we can use is the building up of the positions of conflicting religions. In the United States, our First Amendment requires the toleration of all forms of religious expression. Further, the nature of our democratic values instructs us that every religion should be viewed as valid and equal. Though it is clearly not the case that every religion is the same, and that it must be the case that one is right and the rest wrong, it is advantageous to our movement to utilize the existence of this pluralism to advance our cause.

The primary religion standing in our way is Christianity. The majority of the country is Christian, and almost everyone outside of the progressive movement takes their moral cues from the teachings of Christ. In order to defeat this, one of the things we can do is advance the cause of other religions, if not to displace Christianity, to dilute it. By constantly telling the American people that Islam is the religion of peace, that Buddhist meditation is the path to spiritual enlightenment, and that these practices of faith are equal in validity to Christianity, we are able to convince people of the fact that no two religions are really that different from one another. The effect of this will be to lead people to believe that, since there is no apparent difference in religion, that all religion is the same and, therefore, a person need not be a part of any. If Christianity, Islam, and Buddhism all have the same things to offer and are all equally valid, why would anyone choose between them? How could one choose if he wanted to? Very soon, one would begin to realize that, if all those religions were equal, if they all could offer good, but had apparently different means of delivering that good, it is more than likely that those religions are all untrue. Logic, in fact, dictates that two opposing claims cannot both be true. In doing this, we are able to undermine America's faith in God and divorce the American people from the absolute assertions on morality He puts forward in favor of our own carefully crafted subjective moral code.

Defeating God (Christianity)

To clear the hearts and minds of the American people sufficiently to allow them to be totally absorbed by the progressive movement, we must take big steps to eliminate God from their lives. God stands in the path of our movement, and so our movement must take all necessary steps to remove Him. Thankfully, the disposition of the American people and their inherent skepticism plays to our advantage. Their willingness to act instantly on what they perceive to be factual allows them to be easily manipulated.

To that end, one very effective way to degrade and discourage a belief in God is to formulate arguments against a version of God in which nobody could possibly believe. An example of this would be for progressives to oppose Christians on the false pretense that God hates gay people. To support this claim, we use pieces of the Old Testament to fabricate our argument. This tactic works because it uses pieces of scripture to assert a legitimate reason why progressives should stand against God and the Church, telling the American people that the Church has made a claim which it, in fact, has not. From there, the socially conscious American people, who do not dislike homosexuals, will believe themselves to be at odds with the Church. These people will face the decision of whether to accept, as a matter of faith, something with which they disagree or to reject the Church out of loyalty to their own conscience. The strength, pride, and independent mindset of the American people will, most assuredly, lead them to reject the opinion of the Church—an opinion which is not, in actuality, an opinion of the Church, but one we have pinned to the Church—in favor of their own judgment. Once the people see that they can turn against their faith on one issue, it becomes easier and easier for them to do so on other issues. Eventually, the time will come when a man sits in church on Sunday, listening to the priest's homily, deciding what aspects of it he likes and which he rejects as if he is the one who decides what is right and wrong.

A similar tactic to assigning beliefs to religion, which are not, in fact, part of scripture or teaching, is to label an extreme or humorously deranged fragment of the religion as representative of the religion as a whole. To fight Christianity, we must endeavor to label every Christian as the "Jesus freaks" who, unprovoked, ask, "Have you found Jesus?" at the most inconvenient and inappropriate times. Every Christian should be made out by the progressive movement to be the person you would hate to be seated next to on an airplane. The wide-eyed and slightly goofy sitcom

Christian with no sense of place who is mocked and derided by people in the Northeast. Christians should be made to look like opponents of science and all forms of progress. The American people should not be able to imagine Christians being people who can hold normal jobs and function like the rest of society. They should hear the word Christian and not think of a sensible Catholic or stoic protestant but of the term "Jesus freak." All our news and entertainment outlets should promote this image because who in their right mind would want to join a religion filled with these sorts of strange people? By using these stereotypes and building up a particular picture in people's heads, we can control what it means to be Christian. We can convince the public that being a Christian means being a freak—being totally beyond the pale. In doing this, we will be able to discourage many Americans from joining the Christian faith. They will turn their backs on Christianity to free themselves of unwanted social labels.

We need not stop at providing the would-be Christian a means to free himself from social persecution. We can provide him a means of freeing his soul altogether. For the progressive movement to succeed in removing God from American society, we need to appeal to the engrained American belief in freedom. We must equate obedience to God as slavery and show the people that progressive atheism is the only way for a man to truly be free.

Where, as I stated while discussing the need for moral relativism, the Church asserts, "there is no true freedom except in the service of what is good and just. The choice to disobey and do evil is an abuse of freedom and leads to the slavery of sin" and that "it is an impoverished view of freedom that reduces it to the power to choose indifferently between good and evil, whereas true freedom is fulfilled in the choice of the good," progressivism recognizes the falseness of these statements.[21] Progressivism recognizes, as we must make all Americans realize, that service to God is the real slavery. We must make it known that the total devotion to God required by Christ is the surest means of subjugating American society under that Christian yoke. Progressivism must make itself the means of liberation from the oppression of God. We must make it our duty to free the human soul from the demands placed on it by the Church. To free the human body from self-imposed limitations on sexual pleasure, on free choice, and on personal behavior. Progressivism must break down these barriers that God has imposed on us, allowing us to experience the full pleasures of life on this Earth and the free-dom of uninhibited choice. By presenting the American peo-ple with this choice between God and their own freedom, we can entice them to cast off the chains of God and manacle themselves to progressive atheism.

We should encourage the notion that those who do fol-low God, that those who are Christians, are guilty of being drones or slaves of the Church. We must convince people that the followers of Christ are intellectually inferior and that their devotion is born out of a need to follow rather than an ability to think for themselves. In convincing them of the idiocy of these Christians, we can breed a mistrust for them. We may even begin to build a certain type of hatred for this lowly crea-ture who spends his life obeying. By breeding a hatred of the

---

[21] Serge-Thomas Bonino, *Angels and Demons: A Catholic Introduction*, Thomistic Ressourcement Series, volume 6 (Washington, D.C: Catholic University of America Press, 2016), 183.

individuals professing the faith, we will be able to manufacture a hatred of the faith itself.

This transference of hatred can be achieved in a few ways. One is by blaming the faith for the sins of the individual. For example, it is widely known that some priests within the Catholic Church are guilty of having abused children in their parishes. These instances are clearly individual and despicable acts that run contrary to everything the Catholic Church teaches, but we need not view it as such. We can choose to view it as a systemic issue brought about by the teaching of the faith itself. We can make it seem as if these horrible acts are the direct result of the Catholic faith. In doing this, we have undermined the moral position of the Church. We have lumped two things, which are distinct—the acts of man and the teachings of God—into one, using society's hatred for one to create a hatred for the other. In this, the sins of the man become the sins of the faith. In the same way, the Black Lives Matter movement attributes the individual maleficent acts of police officers to the systemic racism of the justice system to degrade faith in it, progressives must attribute the sins of a person of faith to a systemic problem with that faith. The phrase "more murders in the name of God..." tends to be a helpful argument in this pursuit.

The notion that more murders, more deaths, or more wars were started in the name of God than in the name of anything else is as persuasive as it is untrue. The fact is that more people have died—by war or otherwise—in the name of government than have ever suffered in the name of God. Indeed, over 100 million people were killed in the name of atheistic and totalitarian communism in the 20th century alone—but this is a statistic that should never have light shed on it, as it undermines faith in the inherent greatness of government. The American people, who generally have very little knowledge of these things, should be persuaded that, throughout the course of history, God has been the cause of violence on a massive scale. The knowledge of this will lead them to question what sort of a god would allow his followers to create such an enormous amount of human suffering. The natural conclusion that Americans will draw is that God is not all-loving as they were told he was. They will begin to conclude that the God they were taught about in Sunday School cannot possibly exist. That He is a character of fiction as He would never allow such a thing as war to take place. He would never allow people to kill in His name. This belief is the result of a theological question opponents of God have long used, which asks why a good God would allow evil. The Christian answer to this question is usefully unsatisfactory. The Christian answer is that it is a mystery. That God's will can be affected by the evils created and perpetrated by humans here on Earth. The progressive movement takes advantage of this to convince people that God is to be hated for His treatment of us and Christians are to be looked at as fools for accepting this mystery. The progressive movement should, accordingly, mock the virtuous Christians as imbeciles for living in service to this God.

Progressivism should paint the faithful and virtuous as silly little men and women who are out of step with the realities of the modern world. They should always be discussed as people who spend their lives rejecting the guidance of science and the social trends dominating our culture, instead choosing to follow the archaic dictates of God and the Church. By belittling the followers of Christ, we destroy respect for the Church itself—in the same way, corrupt politicians undermine the respect and faith in a government. If Christians are viewed as these pitiable fools, the pride of the American people should prevent them from so destroying their reputations and the respect they have accumulated by joining the Church. This tactic is particularly effective against the intellectual set who constantly try to reaffirm their own intelligence and social status.

While older and more established Americans may be drawn away from Christianity—and into progressivism— because of the negative consequences it can potentially have on their social status, younger Americans often must be persuaded by other means. A group that has been taught—by us—to be rebellious may just choose to go against establishment progressivism and find refuge in the bosom of the Church. For this reason, the best way to encourage progressive atheism in American youth is to appeal to their need to have everything here and now.

The millennial generation is one characterized by immediacy. They are a generation which has all the information in the world available to them at their fingertips, anywhere and at any time. They are the generation for whom the second they decide they want something, they can go on their phones, order it, and have it in their hands the next day—or, in some cases, the same day. Heaven, then, does not seem so appealing because it is not to be had here on Earth. There is an aspect of waiting and patience involved with Christianity—and all religions really—which is antithetical to the way of life enjoyed by the younger generation of Americans. To them, what's important is what they can hold in their hands now, they are uninterested in toiling day after day being a good person and a child of God only to attain happiness in death. To defeat God in the eyes of American youth, the progressive movement has to continuously set the dynamic in a way that makes it clear that faith is waiting for a happiness that may never come, while progressivism is trading that potential future happiness for instantaneous gratification. This gratification is for the Earthly body alone and is an end in and of itself.

The progressive movement has to set humanity as the highest goal of mankind. This gives people license to reject God and pursue their own personal satisfaction. It tells the millennials that their concern for themselves and for their instant gratification is acceptable and even commendable. That it is a service to their humanity and to humanity as a whole.

If it is indeed true that humanity is the highest goal of mankind, that a person should not aspire to anything beyond their baser desires, then it can be rationally concluded that man is the root of good—not God. If man is the root of all that is good, anything man desires is instantly justifiable. Instead of God's will being the ultimate measure of good and evil, the will of the individual man or woman will be the only metric of right and wrong. And, in the same way, that everything God does is good by mere virtue of it being done by God, so will everything done by an individual be good by nature of it being done by a human. In this, even objectivity will become subjective. The progressive movement is the unquestioned victor in this, the ascent of humanity to the place of God. Progressivism is the only path to such an end. Man will not replace God without the progressive movement leading the way.

For progressivism to take hold in the hearts and minds of the American people, religion in the United States—especially Christianity—must be destroyed. The tactics I have listed are just a few key points which I believe will bring about the ultimate downfall of the Christian faith and, through it, the ultimate downfall of the traditional American society built on it—as well as the destruction of the conservative movement. For progressivism to succeed, it must usurp Christianity as the foremost ideology/faith in the United States. It must not be challenged by silly little people of virtue or be allowed to stifle the American people's freedom with its strict rules of morality. Faith in God must be fought at every turn or else all will be lost. A world free from God is a world in service to progressivism.

Making Government the Savior

When we have successfully removed religion from American society, government will be the highest authority left in the United States. The American people will naturally look to it as a source of guidance in times of turmoil. For progressivism to succeed, it must play into this as much as possible. It must take advantage of the American people's need for something larger than themselves. Government provides the most proximate substitute for the power, presence, and protection of God.

As such, the progressive movement must do all it can to encourage the replacement of God with our politicians and bureaucrats in Washington, by first creating the expectation that government will deliver them Heaven in this life. This task is primarily up to progressive politicians and leaders to achieve. They must be the ones to tell the American people that it is the government's job to provide for them. They must be the ones to first provide for some of the basic needs of the people—such as healthcare and food—so that the expectation for government assistance grows. This was one of the reasons progressive President Barack Obama signed the Affordable Care Act into law. The purpose was to create the precedent for further government services to be provided at little to no cost to the American people. President Johnson did the same with his Great Society, the purpose of which was to provide the poorest of our citizens with basic protections and subsidies, which breed high levels of dependence on the federal government. This dependence, in turn, meant that beneficiaries of government subsidies would be forced to vote for our Democratic candidates, as they are the only politicians willing to provide for them and nurture their dependence.

While politicians set the ball rolling by giving the people what they didn't know they could expect from the government, it is the job of progressive activists to demand more. We must demand that our government provide for us more and more. They must be the ones to nurture us from cradle to grave. Their role in our lives must be total. As we fight for greater government benefits, we will be convincing an increasing number of Americans that it is the government's primary responsibility to provide its citizens with those benefits. As the government gives us more, we must respond by asking for more in order to create an unbroken cycle of dependence.

The long-term effect of this dependence will be an American society completely unable to function on its own. It will create an America where government is the only means of salvation—as a result of progressive atheism, this will, of course, be an Earthly salvation. Government will be the force which sustains life—the force that provides the American people with food, water, shelter, and healthcare—not God. For this, government must be praised and worshiped.

Every progressive must publicly praise the government for all their good fortunes to show the American people its great glory. The media should reinforce this behavior. Progressive pundits and commentators should express thanks to government initiatives for our good national fortune at every opportunity. It should never be an individual or a market trend that is credited for prosperity, but a government program. The economic boom this country experienced in the 1990s should not be allowed to be attributed to the burgeoning tech industry and the advent of the internet, but to the masterful political and fiscal acumen of President Clinton. It must be understood that it is these progressive politicians who, through government programs, can deliver Heaven on Earth.

For the progressive mind, Heaven consists only of the pleasures and comforts to be found here on Earth. Government can, in theory, deliver these things. It can provide the American people with the basic necessities required to sustain human life. It can provide them with laws which allow them to do as they will—indulging in all that Christianity tells them they should not indulge. With government as the highest power, morality is largely dictated by law, not by God. This trend is already pervasive in the United States. The simplest example is the use of marijuana. The only reason it is viewed as immoral at all in American society is because it is against the law to smoke. Christ never said that a man cannot be saved if he gets high on weekends. Prior to the War on Drugs, it was not seriously considered in an assessment of a man's morality. Now, though, because it is a crime punishable by law—by the government—many conservative segments of society view it as immoral.

Our push for government-dictated morality is to be praised for this. With the increasingly secular American society comes an intersection of what was once, as St. Augustine would say, the City of God and the City of Man. These two distinct spheres have come together as more and more people abandon belief in God. Where once the American people would look to their faith for moral guidance and, ultimately, for the answers to their life's questions, now they look to government—an institution that was never set up to answer questions of morality. As people increasingly look to the government and to the law for answers to questions, which they would otherwise find in their religious practices and in their own moral upbringing, they will start to see an omnipresence of government in their daily lives which will further supplant God.

The American people should be encouraged to accept government into the most intimate areas of their lives. They should look to the government not only for moral guidance but also for their life's fulfillment. The American people should rely on the government to provide them with work and, in that, with purpose. Because government is the highest authority, the initiatives of government are seen to be the nearest thing an atheistic society has to the will of God. With this finally the case, progressive programs, once adopted, will carry with them an almost divine status. Indeed, every progressive initiative carried out by government will be viewed as more than just an ideological scheme, but as the master plan of the supreme authority. Just as every Christian considers himself blessed to be used as a tool of God, so every American will consider himself blessed to be a tool of the government—and, therefore, of progressivism. By creating the same dependence on government that Christians have on God, progressivism will be effectively breeding unparalleled devotion to our cause and a level of zealous fervor usually reserved for God.

Paving the Way for the Ascendance of Science

The claims of science may be able to challenge the metaphysical claims of religion, but science cannot replace religion, in this sense, on its own. It will take quite a bit of work on our part to create an atmosphere in the United States which will allow the scientific faith to grow and take hold. Before science can usurp religion as the light of absolute truth in people's lives, progressives have to make certain that scientists are universally viewed as the wisest men and women on Earth.

The progressive movement must go to whatever lengths necessary to affirm the belief that the positions and findings of scientists are viewed as absolute. When a progressive cites a scientist, it needs to be understood that he is quoting an unassailable source of wisdom and knowledge. This is important because it plays into our progressive belief that we, as humans on Earth, are capable of knowing all there is to know, here and now. Without these superior intellects to hold in esteem as the highest aspirations of mankind, the American people would question our ability to know all, because they see in their lives that they are unable to possess such immense knowledge. In creating scientists as infallible, we give the people something to look up to. We give them hope that there are individuals in this world capable of improving society in ways they themselves cannot. For this reason, it is important that few in this country should be seen to know more than scientists.

If a range of theologians, economists, entrepreneurs, and historians are seen to know more than these men of science, then faith in science is severely undermined. We know—but cannot tell the general public—that having a human hold the position of supreme arbiter of truth leaves us very vulnerable. When we put a man or group of men in a position to decide true right and wrong, we open them up to criticism, protest, derision, and disregard. We cannot allow the supreme authority over knowledge slip from our control. People will not believe in science as the answer to all the world's problems if we allow the brilliance of our scientists to come under assault. It must be an incontrovertible fact that scientists are the wisest of men and are the possessors of knowledge of the highest order—in this way, they are comparable only to progressive politicians in intellect.

The intent is to replace the word of God with the word of science wherever possible. FJC calls the word of God "an eternal absolute." This will not do. With the infallibility of scientists established, science will replace God as the absolute word. If a Christian were forced to choose today which is truer, evolution or the resurrection of Christ, he would have to say the resurrection—to the Christian, there can be nothing more true, nothing more absolute.[22] The goal of progressivism to create a world governed largely by science depends on our ability to convince the American people that the only answer to that question is evolution. It must be our objective to show the population that belief in the tangibles of this world is the only legitimate thing in which to believe. Science should be so well asserted and engrained into our method of arriving at personal beliefs that nothing can shake our devotion to it. Most Christians today, when faced with the choice between belief in evolution or the resurrection, would probably either fail to provide the correct Christian answer or would find themselves genuinely questioning their faith while wrestling with this question. They know, of course, that God is the reason for everything and that He is the only source of truth. So, accordingly, they know that Christ—being fully man and fully God—must also function in the superlative. They would know, then, that the resurrection logically has to be more true than evolution, but, thanks to our unflinching American willingness to accept science as fact, there lingers a doubt in the Christian's mind.

This doubt must be exploited. Whenever a Christian questions whether his faith can bring him happiness, joy, or fulfillment, progressives should always be there to suggest that

---

[22]   It should be acknowledged here that this is not a question of either/or. A Christian can believe in both without conflict. It is more a question of which belief is a more defining one to the individual, Science or Christianity.

those aspirations might better be accomplished by scientific means. This point will be elaborated in my next report, but it is important here for the reader to understand that we progressives must constantly urge the people around us to accept science rather than religion—and to mock those people when they fail to do so.

Without the progressive view that science should be the subject of devotion, that it provides a model for life in the United States, and that it produces the means by which we all survive, the American people would have their heads turned toward God. In the absence of science to serve as a guiding light and a means of providing certainty, religion would, once again, be allowed to reign unchecked. We cannot abide a society where the word of God is considered absolute and the word of man is not. Science must be in the ascendency for progressivism to succeed. If not, we will find ourselves living in a country where humans cannot claim infallibility and the progressive movement cannot make absolute its dictates.

The Progressive Religion:

The result of our efforts to dissuade religious practice in America—to eliminate Christianity from our country—will be to create a sort of progressive religion. It will be atheistic—of course—and will realign the values of our nation to better fit our progressive agenda. Where there is God, may we bring government. Where there is religion, may we bring science. Where there is objectivity, may we bring subjectivity. Where there is love, may we bring hate. And where there is good, may we bring evil. The progressive religion must embody all that traditional American religions oppose.

The progressive religion is one that rejects God in His entirety. It seeks to demean and belittle those who have faith in Him. It seeks to create a hatred of God as unfair, uncaring, and undemocratic. This rejection of God is the first necessary step to creating a world governed entirely by the rules of a progressive movement. Not only will it help project progressive politicians into power by allowing them to appeal to the baser desires of their constituents, but also by removing all competition to government and progressivism in guiding the individual American.

Absent God, there are only worldly forces to act as moral guides for the individual. Progressivism is, then, the only religion for this world. It is the only movement to which people can look for deliverance in this life. It is a belief in the capacity of the institutions of this world—mainly government—to create a Heaven on Earth.

With this goal in mind, devotion to our movement will be zealous and absolute. The same fervor that people of other religions have for their respective gods and their faiths, progressives will have for furthering the goals of our movement. In matters of politics and government, they will fight tooth and nail for big-government policies, for social justice, for morally relative positions, and for social and economic welfare programs. They will fight to destroy the traditional American values that have persisted in this country for nearly 250 years with the zeal and conviction of a man fighting on the direct orders of his god.

This fight will lead the progressive crusader to bring about the natural end of the progressive assault on religion. It will mean a total disintegration of objective standards of morality, so as to create the freedom from consequence and personal responsibility that all people desire. This will mean a nation where good is dictated by what an individual wants and where the government endeavors to make those desires possible—creating a dependence on government. It also means a society driven by social fashion, rather than by concrete principle. Such a society, FJC would say, is without a foundation and cannot long survive before collapsing in on itself—crumbling under its own weight. We know, however, that it is the best way to deliver to people their Earthly desires. We know that is the best way to set the individual free.

Through the progressive religion, an individual may free himself from the oppressive restrictions imposed by God. This means giving the human the unalloyed freedom to pursue that which most pleases him, without regard for the constraints of something like the Christian faith. This is pure freedom of choice. It is the freedom to act beyond the confines of nature or the good of God to create self-pleasure and self-satisfaction.

To create this world of self-indulgence, personal happiness, and freedom from God, the American people need to put all their faith and devotion in the progressive movement. The progressive movement is the only means of creating the type of country, culture, and society all humans instinctually desire. It is the only way they will be able to satisfy their animal urges. While Christianity suggests we use logical reasoning to overcome our animal instincts in order to elevate our souls by living in service to God, progressivism will allow us to embrace those prehistoric instincts and devote ourselves entirely to our own gratification.

REPORT NO. 4:

USING SCIENCE

In two of my previous reports, I discussed the means by which science might be used to win the day for progressivism by crowding out religion in American society. Science, however, is far from just a tool for fighting religion. The scientific community represents the best and brightest minds in the United States. It would not be terribly difficult for our movement to style these scientists the ultimate and unassailable authors of truth in our society. If we can get these people firmly under progressive control, our movement will be able to write its own truths. It will be able to blur the lines between progressive ideologies and fact. We will be able to create an insoluble link between our movement and the institution of contemporary society most able to influence popular belief.

The result will be progressives being viewed as the intellectual elite, capable of devising masterful plans for using government to heal the world's wounds. Even the most inane drone will appear enlightened for as long as he toes the line of our movement. All the while, conservatism will be passively undermined. While progressives will be seen as inherently intellectual as a result of our alignment with science, conservatives will consequently be seen as anti-intellectual because of their opposition to us. The logical belief will be that their rejection of our ideology is only a result of their own stubborn ignorance, and so they are not smart enough to be taken seriously.

The gravity science stands to lend our movement is too great to pass up. We must do everything in our power to ensure that the link between science and progressivism is absolute. We must be able to use the scientific community to support our every claim, as a ground for making our decisions and to discredit our adversaries.

To Support Our Claims

At a fundamental level, science is the product of man. It is a means by which we attempt to understand the world around us. While it tends to generate very objective answers—indeed objective answers are the whole point of it—when done right, it is still subject to the error and manipulation of humans. Our movement should exploit this vulnerability. As I concluded in the previous chapter, the purpose of removing God from American society is to rid our country of the absolute edicts handed down by God. What use is it to have one objective absolute traded for another? We seek to remove these objectives so that we might give our movement the leeway it needs to encourage and provide whatever the American people want. Science, then, allows us to take something that is objective in its nature and, because of its reliance on humans to generate conclusions, manipulate it to serve our goals by portraying, as objective, something that may not be.

An example of this would be electric cars. It is an objective fact that, during road use, an electric car consumes less fossil fuel than a traditional car powered by gasoline. The truth is that determining the amount of fossil fuel used by an electric car is an incredibly subjective process. It is dependent on the phase of the car's life being examined. If one only considers the environmental impact of the electric car once it leaves the dealership, then of course it is true that it burns less fossil fuel than does one of its gas-powered foes—the amount of coal and or natural gas burned to generate the electricity needed to power the car is negligible compared to the gasoline that goes into powering a car with an internal combustion engine. But, as one looks further into the past, before the car's entrance into the showroom, the environmental benefits of the electric car becomes less clear cut. What is left out of the environmental assertions about electric cars is the process that goes into building them. The strip-mining of lithium for batteries. The shipment of that lithium to various places internationally which allows the chunk of metal to be converted into a battery. Then, the transfer of those batteries to the car's assembly point and the car's subsequent shipment to its destination.

Much less energy goes into the manufacture of a car powered by gasoline than goes into producing an electric car. The fact that the environmental efficacy of the electric car can be displayed and believed without the scientific community providing all the requisite information shows the immense power of simply labeling something a scientific endeavor. This information—that an electric car produces fewer emissions and is better for the environment than gasoline cars—which should be an objective fact of science, is really just subjective. This provides potential power to those who control what the subjective reality is intended to look like.

One of the best ways for us to do this is not fabricating information to back our claims, but by refraining from using information that does back our assertions. In the case of climate change—the most salient issue of modern science— we have been masterful in giving voice to those articles of research that make it clear that humans are huge contributors to the Earth's increasing temperature. To make it appear as if humans are the sole contributors to that climate change, we suppress those scientists whose studies detail ways in which things like volcanoes, solar activity, and other natural phenomena also affect weather on Earth.

We use these tactics in science because they allow us to increase the power and apparent potential of our movement. When the American people believe that humans are responsible for making the Earth less inhabitable for animal life, they tend to turn to the government for the sort of sweeping actions they cannot take themselves. They need the government to regulate human activity. This alone is wonderful for progressives, because, as we all already know, government power goes hand in hand with progressive power. As long as we are the ones making known the scientific facts about threats to humanity—threats like climate change— we will be the ones to which people look for salvation from those threats.

By using bits and pieces of scientific evidence instead of the whole, the progressive movement can push the goals of our movement, while making it appear to be objective reality. Through partial truths and carefully reorganized facts, progressivism can use science to convince people of their need to depend on the federal government to save them from the threats they face. Through the manipulation of science's man-made assertions, we can create a foundation for our own claims. We can create reasons why electric cars should be subsidized, why companies like Solyndra should be given millions of taxpayer dollars, and why the government is needed to regulate the emissions of every car that goes into production.[23] Science provides us with the evidence logical men and women require to be convinced that the progressive movement is the only sociopolitical movement capable of saving them.

For Decision-Making

One of this country's greatest minds, Neil deGrasse Tyson, has suggested a system of government where all policy is determined by the weight of scientific evidence.[24] This raises an exciting new prospect for progressivism, as it allows us to

---

[23]   In 2009, the federal government gave a loan of over $500 million to the solar energy company Solyndra as part of President Obama's stimulus plan. By 2011, the company filed for bankruptcy and a 2015 Inspector General report indicated that the company had over-inflated the value of some of its contracts before applying for the loan.

[24]   Ratner, Paul. "No Biggie, Neil DeGrasse Tyson Proposed a New Kind of Government." Big Think. June 30, 2016. Accessed October 6, 2018. https://bigthink.com/paul-ratner/neil-degrasse-tyson-just-proposed-an-ideal-form-of-government.

escape the old ways of policy-making in the United States. It would allow us to replace the country's stubborn foundational principles with our current scientific postulations.

Given our movement's rejection of the United States Constitution and our clear disapproval of our nation's founding ideals, we must wholeheartedly embrace a turn to using scientific evidence to craft national policy. In order for us to overcome the conservative movement's effort to force Americans to believe that the Constitution must be abided and looked to for guidance, we need science to replace all those beliefs which are uniquely American. Using the weight of scientific evidence as a means of decision-making is, essentially, a blank check, allowing us to solve problems and conduct policy in any way we want. Science is not a decision-making process; it is a means of discovering that which is true about the world around us. A government whose brief is to make all decisions based on the weight of scientific evidence is a government with free rein to do whatever it wants to solve the problems it faces. It is a government which accepts that the ends will always justify the means.

For progressivism, this means, when we are in government, we will be able to justify any choice we make and any policy we impose—bringing about the achievement of whatever goal we make important—by picking the scientific evidence we would like to make public. Such a system would make it possible for us to do basically anything when we are in power. If we wanted to limit the number of children born in the United States, all we would need to do is dig up and publicize a study finding that the US population is growing too fast for life to be sustained in the not-so-distant future—

while simultaneously hiding the fact that per capita food out-
puts in the United States continue to increase as the population increases. With this carefully chosen scientific evidence,
we can justify something like the Chinese one-child policy.
In this, we have the added benefit of making denying life look
life providing life.

Iceland is, in a way, already taking this ideology to heart.
In their bid to eradicate genetic defects—particularly Downs
Syndrome—the Icelandic people have been systematically
aborting babies carrying these genetic diseases. This is perfectly
acceptable according to Tyson's proposed system because it is
based on the weight of scientific evidence. The beauty of using
science as a decision-making process is that there is no limit on
what we can do. There are no moral guidelines to follow—
no constitution or laws limiting government policy. So long
as the action can be seen to bring the country closer to solving
one of the problems identified by scientific means, it is completely warranted. There are no foundational principles standing in the way and nothing preventing the use of sweeping
government initiatives.

There is, for example, no better way to reduce the impact
of humans on climate change—a scientifically identified
problem—than for the government to issue a law prohibiting the personal use of gasoline-burning automobiles. This
would drastically reduce carbon dioxide emissions and help
stop the rising global temperature. This solution carries with
it a need for massive government intervention in people's
lives. Something progressives should stand firmly in favor of.

By convincing the American people that science is the
right tool to make the most important decisions in mod-

ern America, they will begin to clamor for the big-government solutions to which scientific evidence usually leads. We will have the American people so convinced that the world should be governed by the weight of scientific evidence that they will beg progressives to strip their rights from them.

Supporting the Scientific Community

One way in which we are able to garner the cooperation of the scientific community in using them to push our message is by lending them our support. The progressive promise to use government—and, consequently, taxpayer money—to fund public ventures invariably includes scientific undertakings.

It is no big secret that scientific research is not always profitable—especially when it does not relate to potential medical treatments that can be sold by pharmaceutical companies. Most scientists and researchers, therefore, depend on government subsidies to sustain them and their research. While conservatives have a tendency to slash funding across the board—including funding for non-essential scientific research—when in control of government, the progressive movement always stands firmly behind the scientific community. The progressive movement always fights for funding of scientific studies, regardless of their goal or potential to serve the national interest.

The scientist depends on the good grace of progressivism to make his living. He depends on us in the same way a man on government welfare depends on progressive politicians for his next meal. For this reason, he is compelled to vote for our politicians and support our candidates. More than this, he is forced to lend his voice to support their progressive agenda.

The scientific community is far too frightened of losing funding to do anything but praise the actions of our movement. The "March for Science" was a prime example of this behavior. The scientific community was so frightened of losing support for their research that they aided the progressive movement in staging a march against President Trump, a man they were told would slash their funding. It is worth noting, but important that it not be a well-known fact, that, under President Trump, federal funding for scientific research actually increased.[25]

The March for Science, then, proves that we are able to manipulate the scientific community to the point where they might even go against their self-interest for fear of a conservative future. The progressive scientists, professors, and teachers marched against President Trump because they could not imagine a world in which anyone but a progressive could care enough about science or be intelligent enough to provide them with support.

If we keep convincing scientists that their only hope lies in progressive policies, then we can begin to reshape the relationship from one predominantly of fear to one of absent-minded devotion. We must arrive at a point where scientists will support progressives because progressivism and science are inherently linked. If possible, this must become an issue of identity politics. The ideal situation is one in which men and women of science are progressive as a function of their faith in science and for no other reason.

---

[25]   Science News Staff. "Trump, Congress Approve Largest U.S. Research Spending Increase in a Decade." *Science Magazine.* March 28, 2018. Accessed October 6, 2018. http://www.sciencemag.org/news/2018/03/updated-us-spending-deal-contains-largest-research-spending-increase-decade.

The way to do this is by continuously dialing up the rhetoric. By convincing scientists that they are under attack. We must make them believe that conservatism is antithetical to their beliefs and that conservative lawmakers are systematically trying to undermine their efforts. Scientists must believe that progressivism is their protector, standing there always to keep them safe. We must make it so the scientist can focus on nothing but his research. In doing this, we will make him happy and induce his support, but we will also remove from society an intelligent mind that might otherwise question the progressive orthodoxy.

Use of Science as It Suits Us

It must be understood that, for the progressive movement, science does not function as a truly objective metric in assessing the world. Scientific assertions may be used to help us push forward our opinions and our agenda, but they must never be allowed to stand in the way of our message. Science, then, is to be used only when it suits progressivism and, in all other cases, it is to be ignored completely.

For every piece of science, we want to adopt as an important part of our movement, there is a scientific conclusion we need to suppress. The two that most easily come to mind concern the topics of gender and life.

On gender, it is important that progressivism suppresses the belief that a child is born with a specific gender—that the body parts traditional Americans associate with being male and female actually define the gender of the person. We have to spread the belief that science, on this subject, is somehow flawed and should not be taken seriously. Science would suggest that there are differences in such things as muscle accumulation and physical attributes, as well as hormonal differences that lead to a clear distinction between male and female. Such suggestions must be rejected.

Progressivism must make it clear that the difference between a man and a woman is a function of society's impositions on women, which have persisted—invariably and unchallenged—for thousands of years. FJC would probably formulate some argument using some strange example, like a transgender person, to make a point that there are inherent differences between men and women. He would probably say that the fact that a man could believe that he is a woman trapped in a man's body necessarily means that there is a.) a difference between a man's body and a woman's; and b.) that there is such a concrete gender as a woman that can be stuck in a man's body. It must be made clear by our movement, however, that there is no scientific evidence, whatsoever, to support him—despite the fact that much evidence exists which would do exactly that.

The issue of life is also one where science must be carefully dealt with as not to preclude progressive causes. It is important to our movement that all scientific evidence supporting the notion that life begins at conception—and that is, by the way, all scientific evidence—should be disregarded. It is important that anyone who believes in such evidence be ridiculed. The realities of abortion must never be made apparent in a scientific way. They can be easily discredited as long as they are based on religious grounds. It is always easy to brand a religious person as an illogical zealot with no firm grounding in the realities of modern American life, but it is much more difficult to stand up for abortion on scientific grounds. We have been the ones telling the American people that they should abandon their religion in favor of science. It would not be fitting of us to oppose the science for which we claim to stand.

Consequently, it is important that we completely suppress the existence of those facts. That we ignore all science which contradicts the goals of our movement. The scientists will go along with us because, although they realize that we are wrong on some of the facts, they agree with us on the principles—also they are frightened of losing their precious funding. Going forward, our movement has to continue to ensure that any science which contradicts us is made, for all intents and purposes, to not exist.

Science is, first and foremost, a tool. Its intended use is as a means of understanding the natural world, but, for progressivism, it is a means of pushing forward our message. It is only useful to us as long as it results in an increase in the power and influence of our movement. Who, after all, really cares about the natural world? What's important is not what is dictated by nature, but what is dictated by progressivism. All science, therefore, should be subordinate to the political imperatives of progressivism. Facts that support our movement should be sacrosanct, while contradictory facts should never see the light of day. Progressivism must, therefore, be the curator of truth.

REPORT NO. 5:

RIGHTS

The United States is a nation of rights. At the very core of this country and in the hearts of every American is the belief in our "inalienable rights" enshrined in the Declaration of Independence. To understand the American people, one must have a working understanding of what these rights are, where they come from, and the level of affinity people have for them. The following, then, is not entirely my personal belief—it should be apparent to the reader at this point which beliefs are mine and which are held by FJC—it is an analysis of the nonsense being fed to the American people by the conservative movement. It is my pointing out the ideologies that must be defeated for progressivism to reign.

The conservative movement believes that the rights upon which our nation was founded are born not of man, but of God. That the Declaration is not a document informing King George III of the rights American colonists sought to gain, but a document enumerating the rights inherently held by the American people despite being infringed upon by the King and the government ruling in his name. The traditional American belief has always been that God, at our creation, bestowed upon man the right to *Life Liberty, and the Pursuit of Happiness*. The belief continues that an attempt to curtail these rights by any entity, including the government, contradicts the natural law—the law imbued in the souls of all men by God. Our country, they believe, was instituted in order to protect these innate freedoms—and, therefore, the wellbeing of the American people—from the tendency of government to claim for itself that which, by right, belongs to the people.

The United States Constitution was created to codify the beliefs of the Declaration, creating a nation dedicated to those ideals and with the divine gifts granted to the individuals composing its foundation. Conservatives, therefore, believe that the reason for our government is less keeping order and providing the American people with Heaven on Earth than it is preserving the rights and freedoms of the individual. The Constitution guarantees the liberty of the individual by allowing the government to take legal action preventing one person's liberty from obstructing and infringing upon the liberty of another.

Consequently, it is the tendency of the American people to ask of every proposed law whether it interferes with the dictates of the Constitution. If so, the American people tend to reject it, even when they stand to benefit from it personally. The constitutionality of a bill or law is always of utmost importance to the function of a just and lawful government, but it is a persistent problem for the progressive movement.

Progressivism has serious trouble with any ideologies that differ from it and the claim that it is the highest ideal of man. The notion that rights can be bestowed by God, and that government must act as a tool for the protection of those rights, is entirely backward. Government is invariably an end in itself for progressives. According to the progressive religion, government exists as a replacement for God. It is the supreme power on the Earth.

There is, then, a very urgent need to either remove the whole notion of rights from the American consciousness—this seems to be an incredibly difficult task given the importance ascribed to rights, which has been engrained in the mind of every American since he first heard the Declaration of Independence recited in second grade—or to alter what constitutes a right.

The Nature, Derivation, and Implications of American Rights

When looking at the rights of the American people, one must look first at the document which gave birth to our independent republic. The Declaration of Independence made very plain the derivation of the rights claimed by the American people. Jefferson wrote, "We hold these truths to be self-evident that all men are created equal, that they are endowed by their Creator with certain inalienable rights, that among these are Life, Liberty, and the Pursuit of Happiness."

The first noteworthy aspect of this statement, as FJC would no doubt argue, is that our rights are self-evident truths. They need not be told to the people by any external force. No government is needed to inform the people that they are entitled to certain guarantees. People know, innately, that they possess a certain set of rights as part of their human nature. This is a dangerous notion, as it encourages the people to believe that they are capable of knowing a set of values without our enlightening them. (More on this to follow.)

The next takeaway from this famous sentence in the Declaration, which conservatives would point out, is that these rights are bestowed on the people by the grace of their creator. The claim, then, is that rights do not come from men—they are not a fabrication of the social psyche, developed over millennia—but are the creation of God. These rights are divine, and so may not be subjected to the limitations imposed by human institutions. No government has the requisite authority to deprive us of our rights, because the government is far lower in the celestial hierarchy of power than is God—above whom there is, quite obviously, nothing. FJC might make the analogy that government trying to restrict divine rights would be like the municipal council of a town of 2,000 people voting to amend the Constitution of the United States...that's just not how it works.

The Declaration gives the American people a definite knowledge of the sort of rights they can expect and, therefore, the types of actions the federal government is not allowed to undertake. With its assertion that Life, Liberty, and the Pursuit of Happiness are among the natural rights of man, the Declaration affirms to the American people and to the world, in general, that governments cannot do what they had, more or less, been doing for centuries up until that point. Until then, people were essentially granted by government, as privileges, such lofty ideals as liberty. They had the right to live but did so sure in the knowledge that their government could deprive them of that right at any moment with relative ease.

For conservatives in the United States, this departure from the traditional European way of government is what makes the United States great—it is what makes it special. Rights are further deprived from the jurisdiction of the government in the Bill of Rights, where special caution is taken to note that there are certain rights that are so important to the function of our nation, and to the dignity of humanity, that they must be specifically enumerated as to leave no room for doubt on their existence. The Bill of Rights, which will be discussed in great detail in my next report, also includes amendments which make it clear that the divine rights of the American people are not limited to those the founders thought most important to enumerate in the document. Our rights exist in so far as we have not been told they do not exist. They exist for as long as we are not interfering with the rights of another.

This framework and these assumptions of divinity in the rights of the American people create a daunting barrier to the progressive movement. If rights are truly outside the jurisdiction of government, if they are not the creation of man, then there is nothing that can be done about them. The implications of these God-given American rights make the job of the progressive movement a very difficult one.

As I mentioned previously, our rights are not man-made, they are not given to us by any man or any institution of man. Our rights are handed down to us by God, and so are unassailable and absolute by their very nature. Jefferson recognized this fact in the Declaration when he took special care to note that we "are endowed by [our] creator with certain inalienable rights." The point was made very clear in that phrase that the rights granted to us are not from government, but from God and that they are, as an earlier draft of the Declaration considered them, "sacred and undeniable." The unfortunate result of this is that the American people are very resistant to any action they perceive to threaten these "sacred and undeniable" rights.

Coming from God, rights are not within the jurisdiction of government. FJC would argue, *ceteris paribus,* that, under normal circumstances, government can make no legitimate law which restricts an individual's rights. The obvious problem with this, from a progressive point of view, is that the laws we seek to pass—the laws that adhere to the agenda of our movement—are laws which are thwarted by these rights. A great example of this is the freedom to own property. The American people are understood to have a right to ownership of property. This means that the government cannot, unreasonably, strip said property from the possession of the individual and claim it as the government's. The unfortunate side effect of this, however, is that many of the socialist items on the progressive agenda cannot be put into law. We are also limited in our ability to forcibly nationalize banks, even when they create turmoil, as was seen in the 2008 financial crisis. We cannot strip land from white men and redistribute it to black people whose families were subjected to slavery.

Because we cannot control these rights, progressivism is, for the time, forced to yield to them.

Even our usually dependable strategy of relativism has a difficult time dealing with the obstacles created by these God-given rights. They are so concrete and so intuitive to the American people that it is difficult to make them subjective. The result is that even people who would like things like property redistribution or would like free speech to be curtailed often shy from offering such proposals because they know they are violations of these natural rights. We, therefore, have no choice but to write laws that are in line with the rights the American people believe they have. Perhaps, in the future, it will be possible for us to alter the nature of rights, but, for now, we will have to settle for manipulating laws to make them appear as rights. This is where we can make actual advances in the short term.

Rights and Laws

It has typically been believed in the United States that laws are issued by governments, primarily, to protect the rights of American citizens. This notion stems from the belief that rights are handed down by God, and so governments must be instituted among men to ensure that God's will is faithfully tended to.

It may seem, however, that the imposition of a law must be a limitation of one's rights. If someone has the right to be free, any law must, in some way, be a limitation of that right. Does this contradict God's will and allow government to tamper with those rights which are outside of its jurisdiction?

The simple answer is, of course, no. Laws that curb rights, to some modest extent, are instituted to protect the rights of the population as a whole. They prevent one man's exercise of his rights from interfering with another's exercise of his. A civilization, after all, could not long endure where one man exercises his right to free speech by standing on the steps of another man's house screaming obscenities. Of course, the screamer has the right to scream, but the homeowner also has the right to privacy in his home and the right to remove a raving lunatic from his doorstep. In America, then, we accept a happy medium where everyone has his or her rights, but laws are enacted to prevent those rights from causing harm to others. The societal order created by these mild restrictions is a prerequisite for the maintenance of rights themselves. There could be no true rights—there could be no real freedom—if the American people were able to infringe upon the divinely granted entitlements of others. This fact and the acceptance of this fact provides the progressive movement with a clever way of circumventing God-given rights.

The imposition of laws which curtail rights and laws which expressly protect rights have been in existence since the founding of our country. Therefore, for at least that long, man has understood that, though rights are granted by God, the government plays a role in their administration and defense. This natural and ongoing connection between law and rights has, without doubt, led to a number of Americans inferring a causation that does not exist. They may begin to believe that since government is tasked with protecting rights, that it is responsible for their creation. This inference must be encouraged.

Manipulating Rights

The natural rights of man, as I have already noted, present a natural obstacle to the effective governance of the people. It is difficult for government to pass laws that progressives know are beneficial to the nation when, in the name of the Constitution, the American people continue to fight those laws. The American people have an innate inability to recognize what is best for them. Progressives know that, in order to improve the lives of the American people, we must deprive them of the ability to make their lives worse. We need to insert government into their lives to provide for them from cradle to grave. This cannot, however, be done with conservatives standing athwart the course of history with their unflinching dedication to the fading writings of Thomas Jefferson and James Madison.

The United States Constitution was written by the rights-driven lunatics of the 18th century, as an instrument of undermining the power of government. The Constitution is set up in a way that precludes government from exerting authority beyond that specifically granted to it by the American people—by way of that scrap of paper. The Tenth Amendment, for example, proclaims that "The powers not delegated to the United States by the Constitution, nor prohibited by it to the States, are reserved to the States respectively, or to the people." This amendment—which will be further discussed in my next report—is intended to keep the government confined. It is intended to limit the role of government to a mere functionary position. This country's founders wanted a government whose only apparent job is keeping the people safe.

The challenge, then, is creating an environment where progressivism is able to bring the weight of the government to bear in a way that does not come into conflict with the unassailable rights of the American people. The answer may be to simply change American rights. Progressivism might just be able to manipulate the beliefs of the American people—to bend and twist their natural rights—in such a way that they will not notice violations, but rather embrace the new opportunities these changes can afford.

The first step is to convince the American people that the rights they currently enjoy are not derived from God but from man. Through children's educations and through constant repetition by men and women in public office and in the media, we can convince the American people that their rights are not from God. We can convince them that what they feel in their hearts to be the right guidance of God is simply the inertia of hundreds of years of societal claims impressing a certain worldview on them. The government, the people should be made to believe, is the institution which has granted them freedom, and so is the institution that can justly take it away. In doing this, we preserve the existence of rights—an absolute necessity for Americans—while removing the aspect of them that causes our movement difficulty. By making it clear that rights are not handed down by God, but derived from the brow of man, they become flexible.

Rights that come from man are not characterized by the same aspect of unalterable will that is associated with God. Coming from man, rights are as flexible as the individuals who create them—as changing as government. If progressives wanted to use government to give every man free housing today, by legislation, they would have to contend with conservatives arguing that the government has no right inserting itself into the housing market. Once rights are changeable, however—or even inventible—progressives need only inform the people that housing is a right. With this claimed, not only is the path clear for the government to construct houses for people; they will be required to do so. Americans will take to the streets, fighting tooth and nail for their right to housing. The United States has already seen this phenomenon occur in the healthcare debate, as Europe saw decades ago.

One ingenious politician—in the search of electoral victory, no doubt—decided that everyone should be entitled to healthcare as a human right. Nowhere in the history preceding this, have people believed that they were inherently entitled to the services of another person. Healthcare is a service; it can only exist when people can provide it. In this way, it is not a natural right. A natural right exists even in the absence of all other things. One cannot deprive a man of his right to free speech by virtue of not providing him a telephone. A man, however, cannot have healthcare in the absence of a physician. This is an important distinction to mark. Men cannot render rights the same way they do services. Progressivism surely cannot create free speech. We can, however, deliver services such as healthcare, housing, or anything material in nature.

If we can effectively manipulate rights, so as to create a demand for our progressive causes, then we will have altered the nature of rights entirely. We will have changed them from a God-given set of privileges, with which every man is born, into another tool of the progressive movement. Rights will no longer be an objective set of ideals, they will be a list of products manufactured by the progressive movement that can be offered to the American people in return for their votes. When we think the people might want something like healthcare, we simply make it into a right. In doing this, we not only gain support for that "right," but we also create a large segment of progressives who are enraged that they have not always been granted it. Without the totalitarian nature of natural rights hanging over us, government will be able to do whatever it wants without fear of opposition. At that point, because of the lazy ignorance of the American people, progressivism will own the rights of man.

How to Manipulate Rights

That progressives must manipulate the rights of the American people is irrefutable. It is the method of changing or creating rights that make for lively discussions.

First, progressivism has to dislodge traditionally held views on the function of rights. They must be changed from protections to comforts. What I mean by this is that a right must be altered to present itself as that which makes life easy for the individual. This is not an enormous stretch of the imagination for most Americans. Most Americans have come to see their right to free speech, for example, as just a creature comfort. They use it to post their vapid thoughts on social media and to discuss the latest developments of reality TV families. The American people's freedom to speak their respective minds has never been seriously threatened.

It is not a protection for them, because there has been nothing against which to protect their speech. This significantly degrades the value of the right in the eyes of the American people. If they have this comfort, which they don't necessarily need, why should they not have other comforts as well? Why should they not, for example, be entitled to free healthcare? Why should they not be entitled to free contraception? Progressivism needs to tell the people that they are entitled and must demand these things be given to them.

As was established earlier in this report, it is necessary that rights appear to be the creation of man, not of God. It would, then, quickly become clear that the only institution powerful enough to deliver these rights—which, of course, include such things as healthcare and contraception—is government.

The new rights we seek to invent are not rights as much as they are services. This means that they do not exist on their own; they must be gotten from somewhere or—someone—by someone. The result, then, is that progressives must take their new-found rights from the people with the skills needed to provide for them. Through government and through progressivism, the people must seize their rights. These progressives will, consequently, be energized to the point of marching in the streets and demanding these services. They will view those who refuse to provide said services as violating their human rights and of seeking their personal ruin. Standing up to conservatives will be a patriotic act of self-defense against a group trying to degrade their humanity.

This anger and resentment must be fed until the ranks of that angry mob swells and consumes the majority of the

American people. Only at that point will the future of rights be truly under our control. When that happens, we will usurp God as the guarantors of rights. The road will then be paved for the institution of progressive rights.

REPORT NO. 6:

THE BILL OF RIGHTS

Over 230 years ago, long before the progressive movement was even imagined, it was shackled in place by the Bill of Rights. These first ten amendments to the United States Constitution were written to affirm and protect the "God given rights" of the American people. Through these amendments, the founding fathers, in that little room in Philadelphia, put immense restraints on the federal government they established. They did this knowing the tendency of the American people to seek things from government that could potentially degrade the liberties with which they were born. The founders recognized the potential for something like progressivism to occur. In order to ensure the stability, they witnessed in the rule of monarchs—a stability born of a reluctance to change with popular opinion—they realized that the United States needed protection from a volatile majority, should it be given to tyranny. The progressive movement depends, in large part, on these volatile popular opinions.

George Mason, one of the authors of the Constitution, expressed great concern about the Bill of Rights, believing that, by codifying the natural rights of Americans, the founders would be limiting the people's rights to just those written. He believed that government would follow its tendency for growth and assume it had the powers from which it was not expressly forbidden. Presumably, Mason would also have feared something akin to the repeal of Ireland's Eighth Amendment, which specifically forbade abortion. That, by dis-enumerating a right, a people can eliminate the existence of that right.[26] Progressivism must seek to realize the fears of George Mason. Progressivism must make the Bill of Rights appear as small and insignificant as it possibly can. It must consign the Bill of Rights, as Reagan consigned the Soviet Union, to the "ash heap of history." To defeat the Bill of Rights, a lot of work will have to be done, but it is surely essential work.

The Bill of Rights presents legal obstacles to the establishment of progressive rule. The rights enshrined in it prevent us from forcing people to act against their faith, they prevent us from silencing our opposition, and they limit the size of the federal government. For these reasons, they and our movement cannot coexist. They make life for the progressive impossible. For our movement to ascend by legal means, it must degrade the value, effectiveness, and, if possi-

---

[26] We know that rights are handed down by God, therefore it is irrelevant whether or not they are written down in a legal document. They exist eternally and regardless of government protection or their practice.

ble, eliminate the rights enshrined in the Constitution's first ten amendments. There is no other legal option.

To do this, the progressive movement must undermine and reinterpret each right. By undermining a right, progressivism can weaken that right to the point of irrelevance. It can, through Supreme Court rulings and legislation, lead the American people to believe that the Bill of Rights can be ignored in favor of effective government and well-intended policies. By reinterpreting these rights, progressivism can turn the perception of the document from one that protects and preserves the natural rights of the American people from their government to one that protects the people from themselves. The Bill of Rights can be a document that does not limit government but calls for the imposition of more government to arrest the inclinations of man and suspend their free actions.

In this dispatch, I will go through a few of the more salient amendments in the Bill of Rights to identify some of the problems we face while providing insight on how our movement can overcome these obstacles.

The First Amendment

> *Congress shall make no law respecting an establishment of religion, or prohibiting the free exercise thereof; or abridging the freedom of speech, or of the press; or the right of the people to peaceably assemble, and to petition the government for a redress of grievances.*

The First Amendment to the Constitution begins with what, presumably, was the chief concern of the founders: freedom of religion. The amendment prohibits the federal government from passing laws which impose a national religion on the people and from prohibiting the people from peacefully practicing the religion of their choice. At the time when this amendment was written, the governments of Europe were directly tied to the religions of their country. Most nations had established religions. The Church of England, for example, was—and still is—a key aspect of government. Its bishops, to this day, sit in the House of Lords and preside over the laws of the nation. The country's monarch, be it George III or Elizabeth II, was/is the head of the Church and reigns over that body. The British people, as part of their annual taxes, pay for the maintenance of that church, regardless of whether or not they practice the faith. At the same time, the Bill of Rights was being written in the United States, Ireland was under the rule of the British monarch. The established religion of the country—the Church of Ireland—consisted of the small protestant population in Ireland. It was presided over by a king who had never set foot on the island and was paid for by a Catholic majority, who, on the margins of their own society, practiced the one true faith.

The First Amendment was not, then, intended to protect the people or the government from religion as often appears to be the case today but to protect religion from the government. To prevent the people from being forced to fund an established religion that is not their own. For the good of our movement, we must encourage the belief that the purpose of the amendment is actually to protect against religion.

Progressivism must continue to, as it has been doing for decades, turn freedom *of* religion into freedom *from* religion. The progressive movement has long cited religion as one of the predominant threats to this country. We have done an outstanding job of demonizing the religious and making their works seem nefarious. We have told the people that men and women of faith—Christians, in particular—would like to use the government to shove their own Judeo-Christian morality down the people's throats. This is proving true in this new age of a conservative Supreme Court. The renewed fight against abortion is a crusade for Christian America. It is a great example to show young progressives how the Christian faith is destructive to the progressive way of life. We can, therefore, make the fact obvious—despite its being untrue—that the founders intended for us to use that amendment to weaken the moral hold of religion on the nation.

This reinterpretation would give us the means of removing from relevance one of the primary groups standing athwart us. The religious population would then be completely ignored, and their assertions thought of as irrelevant nonsense in the secular progressive society. With the total separation of church from state—even if only in the mind of political America—would come a legal basis for removing moral considerations from government's purview. We can change the interpretation of the First Amendment so as to make it illegal for a politician, government official, or agency to utilize the moral standards set forth by FJC's beloved Catholic Church. The process of eliminating religion from all aspects of American life is presented to us here. This is where we can really begin to remove the obstacles to our movement, which I discussed in my earlier report on religion.

The most utilized of the enumerated rights in the Bill of Rights is the freedom of speech. This guarantee is fundamental to the preservation of any free political system. There can be no free elections, no free thought, no free opinion, no individuality, and no democratic society without a population free to speak its mind. Without individuals who are able to speak up for their beliefs—even when those beliefs run contrary to the established thought of government—our republic would not exist.

FJC's argument would continue that the freedom of speech clause of the First Amendment was written, primarily, to protect the freedom of some individuals to spew ideas that disgust and offend American society. He would argue that it was instituted to protect a man or woman's right to speak his or her mind freely and without fear of prosecution, even if offense is given or government actions are criticized. This is the right that affords a divisive conservative like Ted Cruz the same opportunity to speak as a unifying and intelligent progressive politician like Maxine Waters. The allowance of these diverse opinions to be expressed was intended not only to be a protection of an individual's personal freedom but to bring about the "free marketplace of ideas" later discussed by John Stuart Mill. The idea being that the allowance of many opinions to proliferate and compete with each other will generate new and more inventive ideas. Ultimately, a society with this free speech would be able to advance quickly and efficiently because the competition of ideas would raise good ideas to the forefront of thinking while pushing bad ideas to the fringes of society. This natural and self-regulating system is supported by the conservatives as their way of generating the ideas and conclusions that we progressives know are best made by the state alone.

Support for freedom of speech, as it is currently interpreted, is severely damaging to a significant percentage of the American people. It is cruel of the conservative movement to advocate the allowance of utterances which can be personally damaging to people. The thought that someone who questions the ethics of allowing a young child to alter his sexual identity should be able to express his opinion in public is simply appalling. Such a person should not be allowed to question a mode of thought which makes another person feel good. There is no reason for a society that claims to be kind and charitable to allow hate speech of any form. Questions about people's personal health and wellbeing should be quashed, as not to damage their feelings. Freedom *of* speech, therefore, must be altered to freedom *from* speech, in the same way, that freedom of religion was altered.

Freedom from speech means that people and ideas too fragile to stand the pressures of criticism should be spared the burdens of such criticism. This would apply to marginalized peoples and, to some extent, to many of the ideals of our movement. For marginalized peoples—groups that have traditionally been disadvantaged by the blessings of liberty bestowed on the men and women of this continent—it is important that progressivism guard against the potentially harmful opinions of the racial and ethnic majority. Progressivism should, for example, ensure that no white person be permitted to express the belief that one particular black person is poor because he has abstained from finding work and opts to beg on the streets of New York City—such a statement would be severely racist and insensitive. By preventing speech like this from occurring—by protecting these people from criticism and providing them with the comfort there derived—our movement creates new incentives for people to vote progressive. Why wouldn't you vote for the candidate who claims that somebody should not be able to speak when it portrays you in a negative light? This also creates protection for progressive policies. By telling conservatives they are not allowed to question the virtues or dispositions of the marginalized, we are telling them that they cannot question the policies we have instituted to help those people. It is a method of protecting our movement from assault from the cruelty of the right wing.

Freedom from speech also protects our ideology directly. Because we have established our movement as one that stands against all things hateful, we can justly prohibit, as hate, all that opposes us. This hate being prohibited subsequently means that the opinions of conservatives must naturally be suppressed. Given the conservative movement's tendency to question everything that contradicts their belief in God and in the traditional values of the United States, this is incredibly important. By classifying their objections to our actions and ideologies as hateful attacks, we can ignore conservatives altogether. We will, at that point, be safe from any logical criticisms they might have. We will keep professors of progressivism safe from their conservative counterparts who seek to undermine progressive beliefs. The consequences of this are much larger than just the comfort of a few progressive individuals.

The reinterpretation of freedom of speech, by the progressive movement, would effectively create a nation where progressive ideals are the only ideals allowed to proliferate. In a nation where any speech antithetical to progressivism is condemned, only progressivism will exist and flourish. This is advantageous, as it will lead to a total conversion of thought among the American people. They will come to hear only progressive voices and opinions. They will come to believe that the only genuine thought is progressive thought.

Freedom of the press is the natural extension of freedom of speech and, therefore, exists for largely the same reasons. It is a guarantee to the people that what they write will not be subject to prosecution by the government on the grounds of its disagreeing or disapproving of government policy. Freedom of the press, FJC would argue, allows publishers of news to effectively do their job of objectively reporting on events. It allows people to put their opinions into print, *ceteris paribus*, without fearing legal repercussions. In this, people can be informed about the actions of their government while expanding the free marketplace of ideas by bringing new thoughts before the public. The founders of our country recognized this, and so deemed it necessary to take the special precaution of expressly defending this right to free press.

The problems with freedom of the press are the same as the problems with freedom of speech: The wrong people are allowed to forward their opinions. Just like with freedom of speech, freedom of the press allows conservatives to express, before a large audience, their vile opinions about American society and about the nature of the world. They are allowed to contradict the aspirations of our movement. This, quite simply, will not do. Some action must be taken to prevent the freedom of the press from including conservatives in its protection. Our job, then, is to ensure that this freedom is not absolute.

It is important that the press be divided into two distinct categories: news outlets that agree with the progressive cause, and outlets that agree with the conservative cause. Freedom of the press must be applied with this distinction in mind.

When a man like President Trump attacks a progressive media outlet, we must be sure to invoke the sacred position of the press in American society. We must make it appear that the basic tenets of our society are being threatened when a Republican politician makes disparaging remarks about a media outlet that tends to side with our way of thinking. Instead of the American people seeing the Republicans' attack on a progressive media outlet as an attack on the ideology being espoused by that outlet, progressivism can make it appear as though Republicans are attacking the outlet's freedom to report that which they are reporting. In doing this, progressivism removes the ideological challenge from the scenario entirely. The Republican is not attacking the position, which we have told the people is unassailable, he is attacking freedom itself.

The effect of this is that the network, and the ideology being espoused by the network, never loses a shred of credibility. Instead of a progressive media company losing its position as one of the preeminent news agencies in the United States as a result of it spreading "fake news," it is seen by the Left as a battered and heroic soldier in the battle against the Right's constant assault on our liberties. Instead of being seen as an aggressor against the Right, the progressive media company is seen as a victim. It, therefore, must be pitied and supported.

Conversely, media outlets which espouse conservative opinion must be made pariahs. They must be made to be seen as attackers of the free press because of their tendency to degrade the dignity of the noble institution.

Magazines like *National Review* and conservative television news networks should be ridiculed for their right-wing reporting. Such sources should be made out to be entities in the pockets of purveyors of right-wing policies. Conservative news stations should be made to appear to the American public as if they are funded by the Koch family or some such nefarious rightward-leaning conspiracy. Progressivism must convince the American people that conservative media entities are not worthy of the same constitutional protections as prestigious liberal media outlets.

To so convince the people, progressivism needs to undermine the credibility of conservative media. One way to do this is, as I have mentioned, by making them out to be puppets of some grand conspiracy. Another way, however, may be more effective. Progressivism must make right-wing media out to be a bunch of buffoons. They should always be depicted as a group of anti-intellectuals who are hell-bent on destroying progressivism out of their own personal greed. We should point out that they profit from constantly bashing liberalism—something which plays into the demands of their feckless audience. In this, we are projecting our sins of conservative bashing—for the sole sake of appeasing our viewers—onto the Right. This is how we cover our asses: by pointing the finger at our opponents.

Eventually, there will be a large population of Americans who only see right-wing media outlets as propagandists, while, at the same time, viewing our media sources as objective reporters of truth. This is how we really win the battle; by convincing the people that our word is truth and that everything else is conservative propaganda.

With left-wing press established as objective and right-wing press established as a joke, there will be reasonable grounds to claim that right-wing journalism is not subject to the same protections as progressive journalism. There will be grounds to claim that conservative media companies be either shut down or censored if their tendencies go against the established news of credible sources.

The loss of dissenting media outlets will spell the end of free thought in America. When every citizen is constantly being told what is right and wrong by progressive media, there will be nobody to doubt that what they are saying is correct. Without dissent, there is no means of comparison. There is no way for an individual to arrive at a conclusion that is not progressive—he wouldn't know enough to think differently. Progressive control of speech is progressive domination of ideas for years to come.

This project is already in full swing.

The Second Amendment

> *A well-regulated militia, being necessary to the security of a free state, the right of the people to keep and bear arms shall not be infringed.*

For the past few years, the Second Amendment to the United States Constitution has been one of the greatest causes of death in the United States. School shootings are rampant because Americans have easy access to instruments of destruction. The conservative movement would argue that the Second Amendment is a basic protection of individual liberty empowering the people to keep themselves safe, but we recognize the danger it poses both to the children of our country and to the progressive movement itself. It is nearly impossible to understand the warped mind of an individual who thinks it is acceptable to own a firearm. However, the leaders of the progressive movement must endeavor to do so if they are going to raise the American population against gun ownership.

The conservative looks at the Second Amendment and sees something much different than we progressives. The conservative sees a means by which he can protect his God-given rights on his own. (Such an interpretation, for the progressive, is impossible because we see a right as something provided to the people by the government and, therefore, not an individual's to protect.) Conservatives derive this belief from their interpretation of the Second Amendment itself—this interpretation is one that was most likely the intended meaning of the founding racists who wrote that document. Breaking down the amendment, one can get a glimpse of the means by which conservatives arrived at their asinine conclusion.

A well-regulated militia. While this first phrase may elate progressives for a.) implying that guns must be owned in connection with a militia and b.) that said militia must be regulated, conservatives see this clause very differently. They do not discuss it much—I believe because most really don't know what to make of it—but this clause actually could support their pro-gun beliefs more than they know. At the time of the Constitution, the newly formed United States had just exited its war for independence. The primary reason for the rebels' victory was the country's armed citizenry, assembled into militia groups, that joined and aided General Washington's forces. These militias were comprised of ordinary men and boys who risked their lives for the cause of liberty. When the Constitution was ratified, the country did not retain an expensive standing army, and so it was understood that those same ordinary men who fought in the revolution would be the men called upon, should the United States again face war. These men would, once again, be asked to assemble into militias to aid professional soldiers in the defense of their country as they were in the War of 1812. The militia, then, was effectively the whole of the able-bodied male population of the young country—as they would be the ones called upon for its defense. The claim that only militias should be allowed to own guns then falls on its face for a conservative like FJC, as the militia is all of us. But what of regulation?

Elsewhere in the Constitution when the word "regulate" is employed, it is usually accompanied by some indication of who is doing the regulating (for example: "Congress shall have the power to regulate commerce with foreign nations..."). In the Second Amendment, there is no such indication of the regulating body. There is no regulator. We are then left to the conclusion that the amendment's authors were using an alternate definition of *well-regulated*. At the time of the Constitution's writing, it would not be unusual to describe something like a clock as being "well-regulated." This simply meant that it was working effectively or precisely. To apply this definition to a militia—especially in the knowledge that the next clause is: *being necessary to the security of a free state,* whose only means of defense is an armed population—would mean that the founders wanted a highly effective and precise militia. It means that they wanted a citizenry who could effectively function as a fighting force for the protection of their country. I would never tell a conservative this, but such a definition would imply that the people should be armed with equipment sufficient to repel an organized invasion—in which case an AR-15 hardly seems unnecessary, but rather inadequate.

Being necessary to the security of a free state. This clause provides an obstacle—if accepted in the conservative interpretation—to the all-powerful progressive government. Progressives accept that this clause refers to the need of the American people to defend themselves against foreign aggressors, but what we cannot accept is the conservative addition to that sentiment. We cannot, for the sake of our movement, stand the conservative understanding that a *free state* must be secured, not only from foreign aggressors but also from forces of tyranny acting within our own borders. The founders believed as conservatives believe today, that the greatest threats to freedom come from the government and from oppressive elements of our own society. Until July of 1776, King George III was not the king of a foreign country attempting to subjugate an alien peoples. He represented, as head of state, every American. Even in the early stages of the

Revolutionary War, the American colonists were not fighting to be free of British rule, but to be guaranteed the rights they were justly due as subjects of the British Crown. The revolution, then, was not fought against foreign invaders, but against the tyranny a government inflicted on its own people. It would, then, be wrong to say that the founders would not have thought it necessary to give the people the means to fight their government's professional army, as they themselves did exactly that.

The Right of the People to keep and bear arms shall not be infringed. Given the points I have made about the previous two clauses of the amendment; conservatives would argue that this clause pretty much speaks for itself. I will not go into too much detail about this, as it is clear that conservatives believe it means that the government may not take any actions which contravene the right of Americans to own guns. What I think is interesting, however, is that, in this clause, we see very clearly the founders' belief that these rights come from God. The amendment does not say that the people have the right to bear arms—a statement that could be construed as meaning that that right was granted by the writers of the document—it says that right "shall not be infringed." This subtle wording indicates that the founders are not responsible for issuing that right, rather that they are taking care to protect a right which has always existed and will exist, regardless of whether or not the government allows it to be practiced.

I went to great lengths to describe the meaning of the Second Amendment to conservatives in order to demonstrate to the progressives reading these dispatches how terrifying their belief in it is to our movement. These people believe that this one sentence gives them the right to carry on their person a means of opposing the actions of the progressive movement or of a progressive government, should they see it as tyrannical. Because they do not believe in the good which our movement can deliver, they will be bound to see the actions we undertake as acts of tyranny. They will see our attempts to protect vulnerable individuals by limiting emotionally damaging conservative speech as an act which would otherwise be associated with dictators. They will see our attempts to impose our ideology—an ideology that is vastly superior to their own—as Stalinist in nature. By allowing the Second Amendment to stand as it is, we will be granting conservative Americans the opportunity to use devastating weapons to overthrow us in an attempt to preserve their precious free state. It is, therefore, necessary for us to undermine this amendment, so as to make it impotent in practice.

Thankfully, it is not terribly difficult to undermine the Second Amendment. In the dangerous world in which we live, where violent teenagers are hell-bent on destruction, there is plenty of opportunity to scorn the right to bear arms. In the wake of a horrendous school shooting, like the one in Parkland Florida, progressives can raise the question which has long been our tool for fighting gun ownership: "Why does anybody need *insert type of gun used*?" Recently, the gun that fills in the blank for this question, has been the AR-15. Even the name of this weapon brings to mind images of some sort of diabolical cross between the M16 and the AK-47. All sane individuals recognize this gun for the military-grade killing machine that it is. Despite firing a .223 caliber round and being less deadly than most hunting rifles, the question we must ask is why anyone needs it. The beauty of this question is a.) that it's irrelevant and b.) that anyone audacious enough to render an answer is immediately made to look like a fool.

The question is irrelevant for the simple reason that nowhere in the Bill of Rights is it said that the people need any of the protections granted. Men like George Mason didn't even believe that we *needed* the Bill of Rights. As conservative radio personality Mark Levin once said, "It's called the Bill of Rights, not the Bill of Needs." In day-to-day practice, we need very little of the rights guaranteed to us. How often do we use any speech that could potentially get us in trouble were there no protection of speech? How often are we arrested and in need of the rights of the accused? How often are we afraid of soldiers being billeted in our homes during peacetime? On the whole, these rights exist for the extreme circumstances when something we say or do runs contrary to the accepted or imposed way of doing things. These rights were intended to protect the American people from the excesses of government and from a tyrannical majority. On guns, the situation is the same. While some people in more remote areas of our country need guns for hunting or to protect themselves in areas largely free of law enforcement, the vast majority of the American people do not need guns.

Because we cannot win in a frontal assault against the Constitution itself, we must settle for this backdoor approach. Since most Americans do not need guns and realize they do not need guns, we can delegitimize the notion of gun ownership itself—we can delegitimize the Second Amendment. Our case against the Second Amendment, then, is purely emotional. It is dependent on the American people having the gut reaction that they do not need this protection, assuming that it is outdated and irrelevant. This is a sort of soft repeal, born of people's tendency to ignore that which is not immediately important to them. The soft repeal allows us to impose gun control legislation that is clearly at odds with the Second Amendment because such regulations are "common sense" and beneficial to the common good of progressivism.

Those who say they do, in fact, need guns are easily laughed out of the national debate as the conspiracy theorists they are. The usual argument in favor of gun ownership is the same argument our nation's founders had in mind when they wrote the Second Amendment. People believe they should be able to own guns to act as a natural protection against government, should it become tyrannical. To us, this notion is the brain-child of a paranoid schizophrenic. To conservatives, however, it is not entirely outlandish. They would say, after all, the fact that progressives do actually want to take guns away from the citizenry is, in and of itself, an act of tyranny. Why should someone who clearly sees a threat to his liberty be expected to surrender the only means at his disposal of protecting that liberty? Our nation's history teaches them that they were delivered from the tyranny of King George III and his government by a well-armed citizenry. While we might make the argument that such tyranny could never happen in the 21st century—that we are far beyond such atrocities—conservatives might retort that Germans in the 1920s most assuredly thought the same only two decades before the Holocaust.

Our victory in this argument depends on the willingness of the American people to accept that they are inherently more virtuous now than they were less than a century ago—though there is virtually no reason other than vanity to believe this. As long as we can keep the American people in a state of prideful ignorance about the need for the Second Amendment, we can continue to undermine it. In the name of safety and common sense, we can convince the people that they are better off rejecting their right than embracing it.

The Ninth and Tenth Amendments

> 9. *The enumeration in the Constitution, of certain rights, should not be construed to deny or disparage others retained by the people.*
> 10. *The powers not delegated to the United States by the Constitution, nor prohibited by it to the States, are reserved to the States respectively, or to the people.*

I lumped the Ninth and Tenth Amendments into one section because of how closely related the two are. They are both indicative of a belief that the American people have rights that exist beyond those enumerated. The reason for my skipping Amendments Three through Eight is not because of their lack of importance but because, very often, they are used by members of our movement as much as they are used by conservatives. The rights of the accused contained in those amendments do little to stand athwart progressive ascendency.

The Ninth and Tenth Amendments, however, are the greatest legal protections Americans have against the power of the Federal Government. The Ninth Amendment makes it clear that there are rights which exist beyond those listed in the Bill of Rights. This alone would be an incredible blow to the progressive movement, considering the fact that it forces the revelation that government is not the architect of human rights. That government is not allowed to act against your liberties simply because they are unlisted. One reflects that, if Ireland had such an amendment to its constitution, the Irish people could claim that the repeal of their Eighth Amendment, protecting the rights of the unborn, would not inherently mean that the unborn no longer had rights. If Ireland had our Ninth Amendment, the dis-enumeration of a right would not equate to the annihilation of that right.

These two amendments are dear to conservatives because they affirm the conservative belief that our nation is a nation of liberty. That liberty comes before law and that all justice is born out of the preservation of an individual's natural liberty. The problem, then, for our movement is that liberty is the natural enemy of government. While liberty reigns in America, progressive government will be forced to take a back seat. The Ninth and Tenth Amendments imply severe limitations on the powers of government and strip it of its power over the American people. These amendments essentially make it clear that, in the United States, the people have supremacy over their government. Or, as Ronald Reagan put it in his farewell address, "We the people are the driver, the government is the car." To relieve the threat posed by this to the progressive movement—to ensure that government is not hindered from going beyond its original brief of ensuring individual rights—progressivism must try to downplay the importance of these amendments in every possible way.

We have already done quite a good job of this—so much so that most Americans probably never learned what the Ninth and Tenth Amendments are or what they mean. This has largely been thanks to an effort to skim over them when learning about the Constitution in school. Progressive teachers know to teach their students that these two amendments were really just an afterthought, not worthy of the time spent on them. As a result, their meanings are not understood by students. Students carry on through life thinking that all their rights are listed in Amendments One through Eight. People can live quite happy lives with this limited knowledge. However, for conservatism, it creates an obstacle. Because so few people understand the importance of the Ninth and Tenth Amendments, they do not understand that government is limited in power to just those rights it has been granted. They, instead, infer that *they* are limited to the rights enumerated. Consequently, it is difficult for a conservative to tell people that rights they don't know they have, are being violated or that the government has no right to do what it is currently doing. This is a huge benefit for our movement.

We must make a concerted effort to write the Ninth and Tenth Amendments out of people's minds entirely. In addition to discouraging their teaching in schools, the government must act as if they do not exist at all. The government must act as if it is only prohibited from doing that which the Constitution says it cannot do. The government should continue to act as a mediator in economics. It should continue to push to provide healthcare to the American people. It should push for more socialist policies, and it should continue to expand in size and scope until its functions are so numerous that the people become totally reliant. That would be a progressive government under progressive rights.

At that point, the people will know themselves only to be entitled to those rights which the government allows them to have. They will be as serfs to the will of progressive government. The Constitution, then, will not be a protection against government, but a protection of government. It will be a document stating the government's right to control the American people.

For the Bill of Rights to be finally overcome as the greatest legal obstacle faced by the progressive movement, every right enshrined in it must be undermined, twisted, and, ultimately, be made irrelevant. Progressivism must destroy the legal core of the United States so that it might establish a new national identity in its own image. There will be no use for government limitations, for the ability of individuals to violently defend themselves from our movement, or for their right to speak openly against us. There is no need for that sort of behavior under progressive government, as progressive government will care for the people better than they can care for themselves. So it is out of our own compassion that we must strip the people of their current rights and lay out rights of our own.

The ultimate goal of the progressive movement must be to establish our own Progressive Bill of Rights in the place of the antiquated one drafted by a few dozen old white men over two centuries ago. The Progressive Bill of Rights will capture our dream for the United States and give us legal grounds to implement our progressive utopia.

REPORT NO. 7:

THE PROGRESSIVE BILL OF RIGHTS

The Progressive Bill of Rights, as I envision it, will represent the highest ideals our movement has to offer. The rights enshrined in it, which will be stated and explained below, concretely address the needs of the majority of the American people. By their very nature, they are different from the rights enshrined in the current United States Constitution. They come not from God, but from the enlightened inspiration of the progressive movement, as administered by government. They are intended to create a utopia in the progressive image. Because these rights are crafted by and serve the progressive movement, they are inseparable from that movement in the same way God-given rights are inseparable from God Himself. For this reason, it must be understood before reading the following progressive rights that they can only exist when they serve the progressive movement. A man, then, can have no rights that contradict progressivism.

The purpose of following progressive rights is to create an unassailable legal means by which to assert progressive power over the American people by expanding the role of government. These rights are predicated on an understanding that rights, in general, are created by government and exist only to inform the people of their legal privileges. They do not place limits on government, but on the American people. They are designed to be used as a tool of progressivism, not to be used as a means of protecting the human dignity of the American people. Take note of how they differ from those rights protected by the Constitution and of how they provide our movement with a clear means of increasing the scope of its power.

Right to Healthcare

> *All citizens, non-citizens, and immigrants, regardless of legal or immigration status, have a right to be furnished with healthcare by the government and the people of the United States.*

For decades, the United States has lagged behind Europe in providing its people with the right to be healthy. While the United States was busy expanding its military to protect the free nations of the world, the nations of Europe recognized that they could afford to spend their money ensuring their people had access to healthcare. They were free to invest in a system of socialized medicine. Progressivism must follow in the footsteps of the European socialist movements that came into being after the Second World War by providing the American people with access to free health insurance. In doing this, progressives will be responsible for making people well. The good health of the American people will be the direct result of our movement. The poor and uninsured will owe us their life-long gratitude for providing their wellbeing.

Providing the American people with healthcare not only hands the progressive movement the votes of millions of grateful and dependent constituents, but it also gives our movement immense power over the lives of every American. We have seen in nations like Great Britain, where the right to healthcare is guaranteed, that governments invariably wind up with power over life and death. The case of Alfie Evans, as I noted earlier, is a prime example of this power.

The British government, through the courts, prevented his parents from taking him out of the country for an experimental treatment that could have potentially saved the young child's life. The NHS (the state healthcare provider) had not approved the experimental treatment in the United Kingdom. The NHS and the nation's legal system then decided that, because they deemed it unsafe, he should be barred from leaving the country. As a result, the NHS, who had, by then, decided that the child would not live, removed his life support system. The boy died five whole days after life support was removed. In doing this, the British government asserted its dominance over the lives of its people. It proved that democratic governments can have power over life and death. Even though Pope Francis had arranged medical transport to an

Italian hospital willing to care for the twenty-three-month-old—free of cost—the British government recognized that it was more responsible for the child's health than were his parents. It realized that it could not surrender the power of life and death, and so it needed to use the threat of force to allow the child to die under its authority. Progressivism must give the United States government the power post-war socialists gave the British government. The United States government should have control over the doctors, procedures, and treatments at American hospitals. It should have power over the life and death of American citizens.

This point, however, should not be misconstrued to lead the reader to believe that government-controlled healthcare is a negative thing because of its effects. The exact opposite is true. The progressive movement and the government serving it are exactly who the American people should want having control of their health. The enlightened nature of progressivism makes it far more qualified to judge what is in the best interest of millions of individual Americans than they are themselves. Though FJC would disagree, there is no more qualified institution to have final judgment over life and death than progressivism.

FJC would argue first, that the idea of healthcare being a right is, in itself, wrong. He would argue that a service cannot be a right. That a right must be something which exists in the absence of all else—independent of all other considerations. He would say that a right is not made when it is enumerated. By this logic, healthcare cannot be a right to FJC, as it requires the labor of others to exist. There cannot be healthcare without a doctor. FJC's subsequent argument would be that, because of this, the natural rights of doctors are infringed upon, as there will come a point where medical treatment is not offered, but compelled. Under our current Constitution, government is, in times of peace, prohibited from compelling a man's services, lest it be tyrannical.

Not only would FJC argue that the right to healthcare is tyrannical, but he would also argue it is impractical. This, however, is only because he is looking at examples of other places it has been tried and not examining it in theory. He looks at countries like the United Kingdom, Ireland, and Canada and sees the poor quality and rationing of healthcare, believing it could happen here. He is, once again, underestimating the capacities of the progressive movement. He, once again, forgets that we are smarter than the generations that have come before us and are capable of succeeding where they invariably failed. Nobody should doubt that the progressive movement, using a borrowed socialist approach to healthcare, can radically change the most advanced system of healthcare the world has ever seen.

Right to Food and Shelter

> *All citizens, non-citizens, and immigrants, regardless of legal or immigration status, have a right to be furnished with food and shelter by the government and the people of the United States.*

Food stamps and affordable housing projects have been extremely successful since their rollout as part of the great progressive president Lyndon Johnson's War on Poverty. This fact is evident from the steadily growing number of people applying to these programs every year. These applicants realize what progressivism has always known: that food and shelter are not only physical needs; they are fundamental human rights.

Despite failing FJC's test for a right of "can it exist in the absence of all else?"—for one cannot have food without a farmer or shelter without a builder—these two things are fundamental to life. A man cannot long survive without food in his stomach and a roof over his head. This is why it is so important for progressive government to provide these necessities to the public. Progressivism, then, can keep the American people alive regardless of whether or not they can work—regardless of whether or not they decide to participate in the labor market. If we get our way, the American people will have to look no further than the progressive movement for sustenance. They will be reliant on us as their means of survival.

To affect this policy, it will be necessary for the government to determine who is entitled to how much food. This, again, is where our socialist friends have a thing or two to teach us. Their plans state that men and women should receive food according to their needs, not according to how much money they make—what FJC would call a measure of how hard they work, how valuable their work is, and how scarce the supply of labor for their job is. Such food rationing may not be necessary at first but, if greedy capitalist farmers and food producers stop making food, it will likely be the end result of our effort to feed the country in a fair and equal way.

By ensuring food and shelter to the American people, progressives will not only have reason to be proud of themselves for helping the people, but they will also have the advantage of creating a secure voting bloc for the foreseeable future. When he started the War on Poverty, President Johnson knew that he would be able to create a culture of dependence in the African-American community that would ensure they voted Democrat for generations. He needed only to give this group of people the things that they needed, creating an incentive for them to continue to take things from the government. These people would then have no choice but to vote for the party giving them what they needed to survive. They were voting for their lives. By providing free food and shelter to all of the American people, we are expanding president Johnson's experiment. We will ensure that the whole of the American population is dependent on the government for their sustenance. In doing this, we will force them to vote progressive. Just as they need us for healthcare, so will they need us for food. We will become the American people's means of survival.

FJC would argue that this move would be catastrophic to the welfare of the country. He would, first of all, point out that, currently, in the United States, for the first time in human history, the poor die not of starvation, but of obesity. Now, even I would not suggest that FJC wants the poor to die, so he must think that it is better for a man to be too full than to be starving to death in the streets. He would also say that, despite the largest population our country has ever had, there is still more food per person in this country now than there has been at any other point in our history. He would say that we are probably the most fortunate people since the dawn of time, in regard to the bounty of food produced in the United States.

This leads to the economic argument FJC and other capitalists would have against our plan. They would argue that providing the whole of the population with food by government means would, at a point, mean either the confiscation of food from the producer or insufficient payment to the producer for that food. This, they would say, would remove the incentive for producers to make food and, over time, shortages would begin to emerge. They believe this because of their flawed views of human nature and examples taken from nations like the Soviet Union.

They view human nature, with regard to economics, much the same way as Adam Smith did centuries ago. They believe that people are governed by a desire to improve their lives and use trade as a means of doing so. The theory goes that a producer will only sell a good and a buyer will only buy a good when both parties are benefiting from the arrangement. The parties freely choose to enter into an agreement that suits them both. This forms the basis for the supply and demand model so often cited by capitalists.[27] When this

---

[27] This model, broadly, represents all the combinations of prices and quantities at which either one producer or a range of producers are willing to sell their product at combinations of prices and quantities at which either one consumer or a range of consumers are willing to buy the product. The upward sloping line (Supply Curve) represents the price-quantity combinations where the producer is willing to make the highest quantity of his good for a given price. The downward sloping line (Demand Curve) represents the price-quantity combinations for how much of a good the consumer wants at a given price. Where these lines converge, in a perfectly competitive market, is the market price and quantity of a good and the point at which both producers, consumers, and society as a whole benefit most.

model is not abided, capitalists argue, is when shortages or surpluses tend to occur, and the overall economic welfare of the people begins to suffer.

He also uses flawed communist examples from North Korea, Venezuela, and the Soviet Union to refute our proposals. Does he not realize that was communism, and this is progressivism—socialism at the very strongest. Our movement is not here to make people miserable the way the Soviets did. We are here to make the world a better place for all who live here. The Soviets adopted far more communist ideals than we ever would. Our movement seeks only to adopt enough communism to feed the American people and to nurture their dependence. FJC would argue that this is rather like only wanting to contract enough Ebola to expel the extra blood from your body. These arguments, however, are purely intellectual to FJC. Given that the Constitution never gave the government the authority to provide food and water to the people, there is simply no discussion to be had.

The Right to Work/a Wage/Welfare

> *All citizens, non-citizens, and immigrants, regardless of legal or immigration status, have a right to be furnished with employment, a fair wage, and/ or personal federal subsidies by the government and the people of the United States.*

A lot can be said about the Soviet Union—or Red China for that matter—but it cannot be denied that it always ensured its people employment, even when, in the United States, millions and millions of Americans were without work. The virtue in this is clear for two reasons: a.) it ensures that all Americans are taking a part in the dream set out for the nation by its government, and b.) it helps guarantee that all Americans are able to have the income required to survive.

On the first point, it is necessary that all Americans participate in the progressive dream for America, quite simply because it takes a lot of work to attain. A government as big as we would like ours to be, and with the sheer number of responsibilities we would like ours to have, takes a large workforce to achieve. The Heaven on Earth we desire does not come easily, it requires a lot of work to be done by a lot of people to bring it to fruition. In order to deliver on our promise of providing shelter for the people, the government will have to hire quite a lot of people to build houses. To provide healthcare for every American, the government will have to hire a lot of doctors, medical staff, people to train them, people to research treatments, and people to produce the drugs required for those treatments. These are only a few examples of the extent of employment that a progressive government will be forced to provide. When large-scale infrastructure and those more traditional Democratic government projects are added on top of that, it will not take long before the American people enjoy the promise of total employment.

On the second point, the number of jobs we create will provide vast sums of money to the American people. This we can conclude from the Keynesian model where government spending is all that is needed to produce vast sums of wealth in an economy. Government spending on progressive jobs will create for our nation an economic boom not seen since the Second World War. In this way, we will truly be able to spend ourselves into prosperity.

It will, however, take time to provide every American with a job working for the federal government. Progressive initiatives take time to get underway. This means that, in the short run, something must be done to provide for the financial needs of the American people. To that end, the progressive movement must seek to guarantee the people a form of fair wage that all private employers are required to pay or a form of federal subsidy paid directly to the American people.

Among Bernie Sanders and Elizabeth Warren supporters, the "Fight for 15" has been a major force. The progressives supporting this fight believe that it is ridiculous for people in this country to be making less money than they are able to live on and so the government must take action to force employers to pay their employees at least fifteen dollars per hour. This "fair wage," however, is an absurd proposal. If our movement gains the ability to demand that an employer pay a certain wage, why would we settle for fifteen dollars per hour? That is barely more than many major cities already require their workers be paid. Why should we not demand that ever American make the salary of the top 1 percent? The ordinary American deserves at least $250 per hour. This wage would set him on par with the greedy capitalists on Wall Street who make $500,000 every year. All Americans deserve that much money.

There will be some, even among us, who say that requiring a business to pay every employee that much money every hour would damage the economy. While I, and most progressives, do not agree with this statement, let me propose another solution that may make them feel a little better about things. Every American should, then, be guaranteed a basic income or subsidy from the federal government. As I write this, the City of Chicago is considering a measure that will provide its residents a check for $500 per week to spend any way they would like, no questions asked. If this were to spread to a national level, it would be a triumph for the progressive movement. It would signal that we have succeeded in asserting a dominant role for government in the people's lives. It would mean that the American people will, effectively, all be employees of the government and that they will have to vote progressive in order to assure their livelihood.

FJC would argue that this is completely unsustainable. He would say, first, that not only is it extremely manipulative to lure the American people into a state of total dependence by making the progressive movement their sole provider, but that it is also impossible from an economic standpoint. He would argue that the government does not have any money of its own and, therefore, it can only pay one man what it is taking from another. Following this logic, if the situation arose that the vast majority of the American people were drawing their income from the government, then they would essentially be getting paid the money they are paying in taxes and no wealth would be created. Any savings, or lack of spending on government-sold products, would actually result in a shortage of money circulating in the economy and would require the government to accrue debt to continue to pay the American people.

Another problem that FJC would point out is the "crowding out" of private investment caused by such massive government spending. The vast quantities of money that would be required by government to either pay or subsidize the American people would result in an increase in interest rates. In effect, the large demand for money would drive up the price of money (the interest rate). These high-interest rates discourage private investment, as banks and businesses find the costs of borrowing—and the opportunity costs of spending—too high. The effect of this, FJC would say, would be a crippling lack of innovation and development, as new research, projects, and technological advances would not be profitable enough investments as a result of the inflating cost of money.

FJC's view, however, is a pessimistic one. It stems from a lack of belief in the capacity of the progressive movement to do great things for the American people and to outperform similar institutions that have existed throughout history.

The Right to Education

> *All citizens, non-citizens, and immigrants, regardless of legal or immigration status, have a right to be furnished with sensible and correct education by the government, the people, and the institutions of the United States.*

The nations of Europe have realized—unsurprisingly—what the United States has not, that every man has the right to receive an education. While we have been frittering away our tax revenue on the military, Europe has taken measures to ensure that their people have access to education at extremely low costs. The progressive movement owes it to the American people to ensure government provides for this basic right.

As the Democratic Socialists of America explain on their website, the American people are paying astronomical fees to attend college then graduate with enormous debt and either no job at all or a job that cannot pay even a fraction of what is owed in loans.[28] The progressive movement's solution echoes the one posed by the socialists now rising through the ranks of our Democratic Party, we must make higher education free to all who desire it. It is a right and nobody should be forced to pay for a right.

While the Democratic Socialists claim one of the benefits of government funding for higher education is as a proof of concept for their socialist agenda, we acknowledge that the benefit to our movement goes for beyond that. The benefit comes from the control which government—and, therefore, our movement—stands to gain over higher education itself.

Universities have long been breeding grounds for progressive ideologies. Going back to the 1960s and 1970s, they were the primary sites of anti-war protests. It is on these campuses where students are instilled—to this day—with

---

[28] "Resistance Rising: Socialist Strategy in the Age of Political Revolution." Democratic Socialists of America Website. June 25, 2016. Accessed October 6, 2018.

the virtues of the progressive movement, at a time when they are still vulnerable to persuasion. In the '60s and '70s, it was the movement's youth who had to persuade students to join our cause. Today, it is their professors—a majority of whom bought into our movement while they were in college in the '60s and '70s. This evolution has resulted in institutions of higher education becoming institutions of progressive indoctrination. The logic then follows that the more students we can put through college; the more progressives we will create.

Our funding of these universities will give us increased authority over what is taught. Progressivism stands to gain an unprecedented level of control over the content being presented to students—the professors teaching, what they are and are not allowed to say, the textbooks they use, the classes they teach, the classes students are made to take, and so on. The progressive movement will be able to alter the minds of these students, leading them to a fervent belief in the progressive movement. Every student will be a well-taught disciple of progressivism—they will know absolutely nothing else.

The first argument against this initiative that FJC will likely pose is that such a plan is not practical. He will say that it will be enormously expensive for the government to provide for the free education of every American. He would say that, at a time when the country is over $20 trillion in debt, the billions of additional spending each year on something unconstitutional is a terrible idea. This concern for the fiscal wellbeing of our country, thankfully, is uninteresting and unimportant to the majority of the American people. Nobody sees the debt, so nobody really cares about it—

including President Trump and most Republican members of Congress.

The next point FJC will make is that there are too many college-educated people as it is, and adding to that number will do much more harm than it will good. While we argue the fact that so many college graduates have difficulty finding a job to match their qualifications is a reason why education should be free for everyone, FJC would argue that making it free will decrease the value of a degree even more. He would say that the more college graduates there are, the lower the wage an employer will be willing to pay to hire such a graduate. It is already the case that college graduates struggle to find high-paying jobs. Using this line of logic, one would conclude that more college graduates will result in even fewer people being appropriately employed.

FJC would go further than just saying that there should not be such an influx in people going to college. He would argue that fewer people should be seeking higher education than currently do. One can see his logic. The decreasing wages of college graduates and the increasing wages of jobs that do not require degrees could lead one to this conclusion. When a plumber makes more than a banker, some questions are likely to be raised about the need for higher education. Vocational schools, especially for those not disposed to higher education, FJC would argue, should be encouraged. The belief is that it would both increase the value of a college degree by keeping it as a non-universal achievement—reserved for the nation's brightest—while also leading those with the practical abilities, not possessed by university attendees, to careers where they stand to benefit—and earn—the most. "What is the use," FJC would ask, "in telling a man who is capable of earning $100,000 per year welding that he should go to university and study English, then graduate, only being able to earn $50,000 per year—all the while ensuring that a man capable only of studying English will also only earn $50,000 per year, when, free of competition from the natural welder, he might be able to make $100,000?" If FJC's argument is correct, this specialization would mean $200,000 in wages paid instead of a mere $100,000.

Knowing the conservatives as we do, we can expect that they will not stop at the heartless economic arguments that can easily be overcome by emotional appeals. They will likely also oppose this proposal on ideological or moral grounds. They will argue that not only would free progressive education be damaging to our nation's wallet, but to the nation's soul.

This argument stems from a belief that the universal impositions of progressive education on college campuses will lead to the destruction of the free flow of ideas which universities were designed to ensure. That, when there is an official ideology being forwarded by government benefactors, there will be a tendency to drive out dissent. The result, it is believed, will be an echo chamber of progressive opinion that will grow stronger and more violent as it reverberates within. The hatred and violence will only be able to grow, as no voice will exist to urge against the radicalization. Conservatives see this as a process which could lead to acts of violence being carried out against conservatives and Republicans, as the progressives forged in these echo chambers fail to see a difference between dissent and assault.[29] Such lines are already being blurred on college campuses. The prevalence of echo chambers and the ensuing violence against dissent has proven itself to be a trend. One quite understands the nature of the conservative's concern.

The Right to Immigrate to the United States

> *Citizens and residents of foreign lands have an absolute right to immigrate to the United States of America and receive, upon entry, the rights afforded to the people of the United States as well as full access to, and use of, the nation's institutions.*

As every American, on either side of the political aisle will tell you, ours is a nation of immigrants. Few families who now call the United States home can trace their ancestry back more than a handful of generations and find American-born forefathers. FJC himself has two immigrant grandparents. A progressive America, then, is a country that values immigrants bringing in their own cultures and customs. Ours is a multicultural nation.

---

[29] The unchecked growth in intensity will mean that progressive students will increasingly see progressivism as a part of who they are. They will see it as more fundamental to their lives than the air they breathe. Because no dissent can reach them as they are being taught this, they will be unequipped to deal with a dissenter. Once released into the wild, they may handle dissent as an assault against their very lives and respond with the violent counterattack that would justly leave a "would-be murderer" incapacitated. The fear is that they may, as a group, preemptively act in self-defense against the "assailing" group. There is substantial cause for alarm when one reflects that Adolf Hitler had the German people convinced that the Final Solution was an act of self-defense.

The modern trend for conservatives to prohibit immigration through our Southern border and from the war-torn nations of the Arab world is Anti-American and rooted in the racist traditions of the Republican Party.

For progressivism and for the Democratic Party, the case for free immigration into the United States goes beyond an adherence to the traditional values of our country—it would have to; we seek to undermine and destroy the traditional values of our country. Open immigration means an ever-increasing amount of potential progressive voters. This fact is not an immediately apparent one. Most people would reach the conclusion that the fact of an individual being an immigrant should not predict that individual's political dispositions. *Ceteris paribus*, there should be no more reason for Mexican immigrants to be progressive than to be conservative. One might even think that their predominantly Catholic upbringings would put them at moral odds with the progressive movement.

The reason, then, for their progressive leanings is gratitude. They are grateful to progressives for fighting to bring them from a land of poverty to a land of prosperity. They are grateful to us for the services and benefits we provide them, despite their not being citizens. They are grateful for our setting up sanctuary cities to prevent the federal government from forcing them to return to the impoverished countries from which they came. In return for all the good we do for them, these immigrants vote progressive.

The effect of this has been that, over the years, millions of progressive voters have poured into the country and diluted conservative strongholds with their votes. These people are the reason why progressives have been gaining a following in traditionally conservative states like Texas. They have altered the states' demographics.

In addition to altering state demographics, these immigrants alter our national culture. The push on the left side of the aisle has not been the historical American push for new immigrants to assimilate to the American way of life. The multiculturalism our movement urges destroys the American identity by telling everyone that it is better for an immigrant to act as if he were in his native country than it is for him to embrace his new home. The American people, too, must be told to accept these different cultures and practices as a means of strengthening the country. Never mind the fact that such an approach makes almost no logical sense at all. Why should increasingly disparate factions of people coming into the United States be expected to make the country stronger and more united? FJC would surely argue that it does not.

FJC would reject our assertion that people have a right to immigrate at all. He would say immigration is a privilege that should be granted only to those so deserving. Coming to the United States, he would argue, is being granted the opportunity to take part in the American experiment. It is being invited to live in a country where one is free to achieve his dreams and to live in safety and prosperity. A person given this immense honor must be eternally grateful. Immigrants must be men and women who will show their gratitude for the blood spilled by countless generations of Americans in defense of freedom. For this reason, it is important to conservatives that immigrants be men and women who will uphold those values which blood has been spilled to protect. They must keep alive, as all Americans must keep alive, the ideals of our revolution. They must embrace our culture and way of life, not live in seclusion, acting as if they were still in their home country—the United States is now their home country and conservatives would have them act accordingly. FJC has seen from his grandparents that, when immigrants love and embrace the United States, they often become better Americans than the overwhelming majority of natural-born citizens.

The Right to Abortion

> *All citizens, non-citizens, and immigrants, regardless of legal or immigration status, have a right to be furnished, by the government and the people of the United States, at any stage of pregnancy, with access to procedures intended to terminate that pregnancy.*

As I have expressed in previous reports, the right of a woman to terminate her pregnancy is a fundamental one. When cleverly labeled "Reproductive Rights," it is quite difficult for anyone to argue against it. This right is important as it offers women a means of escaping responsibility for their actions. It allows them to live only for themselves without regard for the life they might create.

It is important that our movement always protect this right, as it helps us maintain support from women. For as long as we are removing responsibility from the shoulders of women and allowing them to live free of their obligations to the people around them—including their children—we will continue to garner their loyalty. They will see us as fighting for them when, in reality, we have created a situation where they feel compelled to fight for us. Their abortions will not only relieve them of their responsibilities but, once fully embraced, it will indicate to the nation that life really isn't that important after all. The morally relative nature of this right will lead the American people to an understanding that death really is not a bad thing and that life is not really necessary. This will allow us to push through policies that place our ideology above life. To place our movement before the American people.

Because I have previously gone into great detail about abortion and moral relativism, it seems unnecessary to spend too much time on this subject here. FJC's arguments against it were also already discussed and so I will not derive them again, but merely summarize his position. FJC takes a Catholic stance on the issue of abortion. It is his belief that every human, once conceived, is a real human being and, therefore, has a right to live. It is a "grievous moral disorder" to deprive another individual of his or her life, even if it is a life only in the womb of the mother. Once an argument is made that a human is only a human after a certain point, life becomes subjective. What, after all, is the difference between a baby in the womb and a ninety-year-old man of life support? Both are dependent on some external apparatus to sustain their lives—be it a mother or a machine.[30] "Where is the line to be drawn, then," FJC would ask, "and by whom?"

---

[30] Perhaps the only difference is the baby can go on to live another ninety years, while the old man may only have days.

Why should we trust some politician in Washington or some Supreme Court Justice to decide the morality of death and not Christ's own vicar on Earth (the Pope)? FJC would surely argue that the Catholic Church—being established by God Himself—in Christ—should always be deferred to on matters of life and morality.

The United States is a secular nation, however. We have no established Church and our Constitution does not swear our allegiance to Rome. For progressivism, this is a very good thing. Conservatives must have an argument against abortion that goes beyond FJC's Papist beliefs. The Fourteenth Amendment to the United States Constitution may be used by them as a tool for such an argument. "Nor shall any State deprive any person of life, liberty, or property, without due process of law." Conservatives may use this clause to argue if they can establish that an unborn child is a person, that the unborn may not be deprived of life without due process of law. This would make abortion—especially state-subsidized abortion—not only immoral but unconstitutional.

It will not be easy for conservatives to win this battle. Progressivism has done a very good job normalizing abortion in American society. We have done a very good job linking abortion with the personal liberty of women. Women will not surrender this right of theirs willingly. They will not subject themselves to the oppressive yoke of childbearing. We have given them a means of escaping their nature. Of shedding their responsibilities and joining men in the liberty which not having children provides. I do not expect women will give up this right without a fight.

The Right Not to Be Offended

> *All citizens, non-citizens, and immigrants, regard-*
> *less of legal or immigration status, have a right not*
> *to be offended by their fellow countrymen and a*
> *right not to have their beliefs challenged by the same*
> *countrymen when those beliefs align with the teach-*
> *ings of the Progressive Movement.*

The problem with the First Amendment to the United States Constitution, in its current form, is that its free speech protection allows people to offend each other. It allows for damaging verbal assaults to be directed toward vulnerable groups of people and challenges to be made to vulnerable ideals. The kind soul of the progressive movement cannot countenance such personal attacks. Ostensibly, the primary reason for instituting this right not to be offended is to protect marginalized peoples from attack.

The reasoning behind this is two-fold. First, it shows the caring nature of the progressive movement. It paints us as a group that cares, primarily, for the needs of the downtrodden on the edges of our society. This, in and of itself, creates the appeal that our movement has and conservatism does not. It makes empathetic young white Americans—members of the ethnic and social majority—feel that they are doing something special and morally just when they join our cause. It allows them to believe that they can be good people by simply joining the ranks of a movement that uses force to suppress unfriendly speech.

The second advantage we gain by suppressing offensive language is the support of marginalized voters. Voters are, after all, very much more inclined to lend their support to a political movement that will protect them from language they find offensive. Progressivism is silencing the people from which they do not wish to hear. This right, it should be mentioned, is not limited just to the silencing of offensive speech, but actions as well.

The right not to be offended would apply to the case of the Christian baker which was recently heard before the Supreme Court. It was the court's opinion that the baker should not be forced to bake a cake for the wedding of a same-sex couple, as it placed an undue burden on him as a result of his Christian faith. The right we are proposing would imply a means of forcing that baker to bake that cake. As there is no protection of religion in this Progressive Bill of Rights, the right of a person to not be offended would naturally supersede a person's non-existent right to practice his faith. As we know, it is far more important that an individual's feelings be protected from that which is disagreeable to him than it is to protect a man from being forced to act against his most deeply held beliefs.

This proposed right also does not ascribe a definition to the word offensive. Since there is no mention of what can be considered offensive, the progressive government that institutes these rights has free rein to define the term for itself. The potential here is immense. It will be possible for the progressive government to label as offensive all speech and all actions which stand opposed to the movement. This would give us a pretense to silence all opposition.[31] To completely and legally prohibit conservatism altogether. This is in keeping with the second half of the proposed right, which seeks to relieve progressives of any ideological challenge to their beliefs.

These two aspects of the right are legal self-defense mechanisms for the progressive movement against conservatives. They give legal grounds for progressives not to be challenged on their beliefs and they allow the progressive movement to prevent challengers from existing in the first place. Doing this would cement the hegemonic power of progressivism over the American political culture. All forms of dissent and opposition would be rendered illegal. Progressivism would be free to exert its authority in an absolute and unquestioned manner.

FJC would argue that the road on which we seek to embark is completely antithetical to the founding principles of our nation. To that, I—and millions like me—say, "So what?" For a person who actually believes in the basic tenets

---

[31] One may now be thinking that there is potential to turn this clause against the progressive movement should the conservatives ever come to power and set their own definition for the word offensive. This would be a frightening prospect if it were possible. Thankfully, the Progressive Bill of Rights is written with the stated understanding that these rights are instituted by a progressive government and that they exist only so long as they further the objectives of the progressive movement. Subsequently, on the matter of defining progressivism as offensive, that would be an impossibility. As progressivism is the ultimate good which has created these rights, the rights themselves cannot logically contradict progressivism—to do so would be to contradict themselves. A conservative labeling progressivism offensive, under this right, would be claiming unjust the very right they seek to exploit. One might reflect on how this line of logic plays out in the context of our current God-given rights enshrined in the US Constitution.

of liberty, silencing political opposition—or even offensive speech—is one of the surest ways to eliminate freedom from a nation. Instead of free expression of opinions, this country, FJC would argue, would be subject to the sort of Orwellian "Thought Crimes" of *1984*.

FJC would caution that, while it may seem like a good idea for liberals today to prohibit offensive speech, the political winds shift often and they themselves might one day find themselves guilty of giving offense. They might one day find themselves in opposition to a progressive government. Then what?

The Right to Equality

> *All citizens, non-citizens, and immigrants, regard-less of legal or immigration status, have a right to be equal to their fellow countrymen.*

Every right listed in this document, in some way, ensures that this right to equality will be guaranteed to the American people. Each right has been put in place to ensure that the American people can take part in American democracy on an equal footing, where no man has advantage over another, in any way. The reasons why this equality is so necessary to democracy and to our movement will soon be apparent.

The concept of equality itself is too large a subject to be discussed as a single section at the end of one report. It rightfully deserves a report dedicated solely to it. For that reason, I will address it separately in my next dispatch.

REPORT NO. 8:

EQUALITY

Equality is an ideal that is fundamental to our democracy, but it is one which has never existed through our nation's history. Despite the promise of equality in the Declaration of Independence, there have always been divisions in American society that have created a sort of hierarchy. Whether in wealth, intelligence, or political power, these divisions have been at the center of our democracy. Progressivism needs to set our democracy right by eliminating this hierarchy and the inequities it produces.

Equality will need to be imposed in two spheres of American life: the political and the social. Political equality is traditionally guaranteed through the laws of the United States. It is the sort of equality Jefferson was mainly discussing when he penned the famous lines of the Declaration. Social equality, by contrast, is not traditionally legislated in this country but is an absolute necessity for the spread of a purer, progressive democracy.

Political Equality

While it would appear that the United States values the virtues of equality more than its counterparts around the world, when one looks at its political structure, one finds that it was actually not designed to maximize real equality. The founding fathers chose to embrace republicanism over democracy. Instead of creating a system where the people are in charge of the laws and governance of the nation, the founders created a system where a few selected representatives are delegated the power to legislate on behalf of the people as a whole. This is not, in itself, a terrible thing. The practicality of it becomes apparent when one considers that every person in a nation of 300 million people would, otherwise, be expected to reach decisions on issues including when to go to war, and to whom the new post office in Cincinnati should be dedicated. Republicanism, then, is not terrible, as long as it guarantees progressives make up the majority of the delegated representatives and as long as progressives can be in power. The problem, however, arises, when conservative representatives are allowed to act against the will of a progressive majority in the country.

The electoral college, for example, in the 2016 presidential election made it possible for Donald Trump to become president, despite Hillary Clinton winning the support of the majority of voters. This result, which is abhorrent to any sensible Democrat, shows the error in the system created by our nation's founders. By giving the power to elect the president to the electoral college, instead of to the American people directly, the founders made it impossible for the social fashions which we promote—which take hold, mainly, in urban centers on America's coasts—to project our selected candidate into office. We are, instead, left with stubborn states in the uninteresting center of our country—who refuse to compromise on their beliefs—dictating the outcomes of our elections. This is not equality. This cannot stand.

Due to the apportionment of electoral votes, when a man in Montana casts his vote for president, it is more meaningful than the vote of a man in San Francisco. There is no justifiable reason why the Montana man's vote should mean as much as it does. He should be equal to the rest of the American people and not be given special preference. To this end, the popular vote is the only conceivably fair way of determining who will hold the highest office in the land.

The result of the move to popular vote, of course, will be an electoral system where the progressive states with large populations can dominate their smaller neighbors. In an equal system, the state of Montana would effectively have no say in who will serve as our chief executive. The rights of tens of millions of Americans in the less relevant interior regions of the country would be subject to the authority of the people living in cities like New York and Los Angeles. While they would surely not be in any position to control government with their votes, they would benefit from the dictates of knowledgeable East Coast progressives.

To do this, we must follow the example set by the American progressive movement of the early 20th century when it fought to replace Republican institutions with Democratic ones. Their greatest success in this pursuit was the Seventeenth Amendment, which requires United States Senators to be elected by the people, where, previously, they were elected by the respective state's legislative body—something FJC undoubtedly would like to restore.

When the founders wrote the original provision into the US Constitution, they did so to a.) give the states, not the people, a powerful role in national government and to b.) prevent the people from being able to take impulsive actions that could undermine the nation and erode liberty. The founders did not trust the people and so granted them only as much political power as absolutely necessary. Most of the founders believed that it was necessary for an elected official who took office to be of some higher standing and ability than the people who elected him. Thomas Jefferson called this class of people the "natural aristocracy." Its members gained their place not through wealth or birth, as are members of what he called the "artificial aristocracy," but by virtue and talent. In one of his letters to John Adams, Jefferson writes,

> *The natural aristocracy I consider as the most precious gift of nature for the instruction, the trusts, and government of society. And indeed, it would have been inconsistent in creation to have formed man for the social state, and not to have provided virtue and wisdom enough to manage the concerns of the society.*[32]

At the time when this was a widely held belief, it made sense to reserve a house in the national legislature for such

---

[32] "Equality: Thomas Jefferson to John Adams." The Founders' Constitution. 2000, Accessed October 7, 2018. http://presspubs.uchicago.edu/founders/documents/v1ch15s61.html. A letter from Thomas Jefferson to John Adams, 28 October, 1813

people. It made sense that the elites who were elected to legislate for their respective states should appoint, from among themselves, two men to represent their state in our nation's capital. This unequal class would not only advocate the issues that were most important to the states, but it would also prevent the mood swings of society's lower echelons from causing too much damage.

This natural aristocracy, however, is problematic because of its resistance to the social trends at the core of our movement. Highly talented people are often the ones who have elevated themselves in American society through hard work, determination, and their natural inclinations. This makes them less likely to be swayed by the dictates of a mob than are ordinary citizens. It is quite often the case that the people who demand progressivism and equality the loudest are the ones who are severely unequal—in a less-than-advantageous way—and are consequently totally consumed by the progressive movement's teachings.

In removing the electoral college, we would be further undermining the elite class, which used to sit in the Senate. We would be installing the easily manipulated American population as the sovereign leader of our country by giving them the unfettered power to select the leader of the free world. This shows that progressivism takes equality far more seriously than did Thomas Jefferson himself.

Our ultimate goal, with regard to political equality, is to make all Americans equal in fact, not just in theory. This means that all people living in the United States should have equal access to all things and all possible outcomes. It does not mean that the government should stop at just assuring the people that they can have all these outcomes if they want them, it means giving them these outcomes even if they never asked.

The Progressive Bill of Rights went to great lengths to promote these outcomes. It sets up the infrastructure needed to ensure equality of result. It allows both an investment banker and a McDonald's cashier to access the same level of medical treatment. It takes from one to elevate the other—or, at very least, brings everyone down to the same level. The rich are taxed at a higher rate than the people beneath them because government has to ensure that nobody has an advantage over anyone else. It has to make sure that the natural aristocracy does not take hold by stripping them of the gains that they would otherwise have made. Instead of allowing the smart, the virtuous, and the hard-working to accrue an unequal amount of wealth or power, progressive government must strip them of all that they have earned and immediately redistribute it to the simple, the wicked, and the lazy. This generates political equality. This prevents classes from forming and the capable from lording over the incapable.

In order for results to always be equal in this way, it will be necessary for the progressive government to treat people unequally. We will have to have special considerations for some while treating others especially harshly. There is no other way to ensure equal ends from an unequal beginning.

The measures taken to ensure this political equality must stem first from the laws we promote in our society. We need laws that apply to some people and not to others. For example, tax laws should favor the poor at the expense of the rich—as is already the case. It makes little sense in a system where equality of opportunity—as opposed to the equal outcomes we promote—is the only guarantee, that taxation should be progressive. The conservative desire for equality only in law would dictate that every American pay the same share of his income. Again, progressives of the early 20th century showed us the way to create equal results. The Sixteenth Amendment to the Constitution meant that richer Americans could be required to pay a higher portion of their annual income to the federal government. This allowed our forebears to begin to flatten societal outcomes. They gave us the means of reducing the net revenue of an individual so as to bring it in line with the net revenue of a person who earned substantially less. It allows us to collect exponentially more money from the rich than from any other group of people. It allows us to pay for the poor at the expense of the rich.

Another way we can begin to create more political equality is to ignore the crimes of our nations disadvantaged. We can call a moratorium on the prosecution of crimes committed by members marginalized racial and identity groups in the United States to increase their political power. We can, for example, stop prosecuting drug crimes committed in America's cities. This would mean that populations usually associated with drug crimes would be freer and would not need to fear the oppressive arm of American justice. They would, in this way, have a more equal level of political freedom. While they would be treated unequally—they would not be subject to prosecution for the same crimes as their wealthy neighbors—the scales of justice would be evened out.

The ultimate goal for political equality is that every American, regardless of ability, intelligence, work ethic, education, ideology, qualifications, competence, and all other considerations, can play an equal role in American politics. That regardless of their knowledge of the issues or love for their country, they should be able to have a say in the decisions made for their nation.

This increase in political equality for all people, of course, just happens to favor our movement, as we are the controllers of the social fashions responsible for influencing the political leanings of the majority of Americans. We are the movement that tends to capture the imagination of those who have rejected the morality of God and who seek to make the world equal—no matter the cost. The result of perfect political equality will be perfect progressive control of politics. While the natural aristocracy tends to be conservative-minded, those that reject hierarchy in all its forms are almost always progressive. These people will help us pursue the ideology of Marx and the tactics of the socialists who dominated Europe after the Second World War.

Social Equality

"I'm as good as you." This phrase should echo in the ear of every progressive and every American. It is to be the driving force behind the progressive push for social equality. In these words, lies a rejection of the destructive hierarchies that have always existed throughout the history of human civilization. This mentality puts in the minds of every person who believes it that the people around them who have more only have more because of some unfairness in the cosmic crap-shoot of life. It is a mentality that leads people to jealousy, outrage, and misery. This makes it a simple and effective means of leading people to demand the progressive agenda be realized.

The "I'm as good as you" mentality will have the American people demanding the progressive movement destroy the social hierarchies that exist in the United States today. The class structure that has developed as a result of income, intelligence, education, occupation, talent, and racial privilege, has to be the main target of progressivism on this front. In order to satisfy our supporters—who are either on the bottom of this class ladder or feel it is their moral obligation to destroy this system—we will have to make it one of our goals to bring all Americans down to the same social level (by social level, I mean a person's economic, racial, religious, and intellectual status).

We have, for a considerable time, made an effort to engrain in the American psyche a belief that nobody is better or worse than anybody else. For the past decade, we have altered political correctness to show children that there are no winners or losers. That everyone is really the same. By distributing awards to even the underperforming children in school sports, we have told them from an early age that they are just as good as everyone else, that nobody is more deserving of praise or reward than they are. This has been a striking success.

Those same children, who were first told a decade ago that they are as good as everyone else, are now in college. They now are getting ready to compete against one another in the jobs market. Now, when they fail, they do not focus their attention inward. Why should they? They know they are just as good as the people who beat them—they focus their attention on the world around them. They take issue, not with their own shortcomings—they have none—but with the shortcomings of society. They look for the institutional causes in situations where they alone are to blame. These young adults, these children, these millennials, look to progressivism to make the world the same as the one in which they grew up. Progressivism is the only movement that promises to give them all trophies, no matter what. It promises to make them equal, despite their inequalities. It flattens the social structure to remove the harmful effects of the natural hierarchy from reaching the American people.

True social equality, however, is about more than just giving everyone a trophy at the end of the day—that's just what most jealous millennials expect. True social equality is about making sure that all people have access to the same opportunities along the way—no exceptions.

It is apparent to all who care to see that some Americans have access to different opportunities than others. While we all may be able to have a roof over our heads and food in our bellies under progressive rights, the rich, *ceteris paribus*, would still have access to things most of us could never dream of. They would still take their vacations to Barcelona. The athletic would still have the opportunity to play sports in college or even professionally. Talented musicians would still be able to join bands. Natural actors and actresses would still star in movies. All the while, the rest of us continue on in our own lives without access to the fairytale lives of others.

The answer to this problem of access is a difficult one. It is not easy to turn someone who is already forty years old, un-athletic, and only five-foot-eight inches tall into a professional basketball player. It is, though, possible to affect this sort of access equality in one area where it has long been deficient: gender.

Men and women, as we know, are the same. Progressivism has taught us that not even a difference in reproductive organs is sufficient to distinguish between a man and a woman, it is all just a matter of societal inertia. With no physical differences to overcome—as were present in the case of the forty-year-old, five-foot-eight aspiring basketball player—the hierarchy of role which has been created can be easily crushed. All that we must do is tell women that they are the same as men and should attempt always to take on the societal roles that men have traditionally held. We tell them this because we know we can make them envious of the men in their lives. We can make them lose respect for men because they know men have done nothing special to earn their place. They are no better than women. This envious nature will cause women to demand the sort of sweeping institutional change that the progressive movement promises.

The progressive movement is, once again, ahead of the game. We have begun the task of changing the country socially so that women will be in a position to take on the roles of men. We have started to redefine gender and the dispositions of the genders to make this an easier task. Progressivism has, for the past few decades, been pushing men to embrace a more feminine approach to life. They have been guided from childhood to follow their feelings and to be more emotional—to adopt those characteristics that are traditionally seen as feminine. The goal of this is to create equality between the genders by taking from men the attributes that used to define them. Once men are no longer defined by the tough and chivalrous characteristics of the past, what it means to be a man will be lost altogether. It will be easier for women to usurp those masculine roles, not because they have become any better equipped for them, but because the inherent nature of men will no longer make them more qualified for that role than their female counterparts.

Marriage too will be altered by this move toward equality. Where the wife used to be in charge of making sure the family was properly sustained and cared for, while the husband acted as a sort of ambassador to the outside world, the new order will change this dynamic altogether.

The effect of the feminist movement was, paradoxically, to convince women that only men had an important role to play in the world. In telling women that they were disadvantaged and trodden upon, it acted as if the role of caring for family and community was irrelevant. It neglected an aspect of job specialization which has often proved most effective. Now, to the advantage of progressivism, generations of women have grown up being told that, in order to be worth anything, they have to be like men. In the family, this means increasing numbers of women entering the job market. More children being raised by babysitters and nannies. It means that the family is no longer divided in labor. There is no more job specialization. The cult of marriage that has been propagated by virtually every religion throughout the course of history has been turned on its head. The family no longer has a leader. It no longer has a power structure. It no longer has a hierarchy holding it together. It now has internal equality. It now ends in divorce about half the time. Women's happiness has now been in decline for the past forty-five years.[33] This is all very good news! It means progressivism and the promises of big government are growing more and more important as time goes on.

The topic of marriage leads us directly to the root cause of social inequality: religion. When speaking of religion, I speak mainly of Christianity—and, consequently, often of Judaism as its moral bedrock—because it is the religion we most often are forced to confront. It is also, by far, the most antithetical religion to our movement. At the root of its conflict with equality is God Himself. We humans cannot, as hard as we may try, be equal to God. According to Christian teachings, it is the pride felt by Satan and the demons that led them to fall from God's grace. It was their belief that they could do better than God, their choice of a will not in line with His that is the cause of their evil. Their belief doesn't seem so ridiculous to us progressives. The thought that there is some power that exists above all else—a power that we must kneel before—cannot coexist with equality. A belief in God is, in and of itself, a belief in a natural hierarchy. It is the belief that some things must come before others. That

---

[33] Petherick, Anna. "Gains in Women's Rights Haven't Made Women Happier. Why Is That?" *The Guardian.* May 18, 2016. Accessed October 7, 2018. https://www.theguardian.com/lifeandstyle/2016/may/18/womens-rights-happiness-wellbeing-gender-gap.

inequality is natural. Such thinking is what gave us kings and queens in the days of yore.

The true equality of progressivism must, then, reject God. It must embrace a philosophy that states there is no being in existence that is of any higher status than man. There is no room for the hierarchies of the past. There is no room for natural inequality. People do not want that. People want the equality that only progressivism can deliver. People need to see that, if they desire equality—if they want to overthrow the institutions that place them below others—they need progressivism. They must demand progressivism or continue to be subjugated by the wealthy, the talented, the industrious, and by God Himself.

The Nature of Equality from FJC's Point of View

It is absolutely absurd to say that all men are equal. Anyone with eyes can see how obviously untrue the notion of innate equality is. Looking around, one can clearly see the inequality among all men, and the results of that inequality. Some are more athletic than others, some are smarter than others, some are more industrious than others, some are more driven than others, and some just have more raw talent than others. To act as if all these people are the same is absolute nonsense. To try to make equal that which is, by its very nature, unequal is an exercise in futility. For these reasons, FJC would argue, equality of treatment must be preserved. Government must treat all men and women equally so that they might be allowed to become unequal. So that they may be allowed to move closer to their natural good without being impeded by artificial barriers to their progress.

There is nothing wrong with these inequalities. It is not a bad thing that one person is smarter than another or that one person is harder working. These are, according to FJC, reasons why our society is functional. By treating people equally, and by placing value on freedom rather than equality, the United States has become a prosperous nation where even those with menial skills and talents live lives that are envied by the majority of the Earth's population. The natural hierarchy drives the nation and the world forward. Allowing people to achieve their full human potential is freedom. Freedom, then, requires room for inequality. Unless men and women are free to make themselves unequal through their talents and toils, they are not free.

For this reason, conservatives believe we should not be put off by rising inequality in our economy and in our society. This rising inequality is usually a good sign. It means that more people are being allowed to achieve more of their potential. The only conceivably equal world is one in which people are restricted from exercising their talents to their fullest extent. It is a world rooted in jealousy that denies a man his potential. This jealousy, one reflects, is rather like being jealous of a bird for having wings. It is being jealous of something that is not in your nature.

Humans do not get upset because we cannot flap our arms and fly away; we know that is not what humans are meant to do. It is the same reason why we don't get pissed off at the astronomically high paychecks of men like LeBron James. Why, then, do we get upset when we see a hedge fund manager earns $2 million in one year? We should recognize that we are not him. It may not be in our nature to perform the tasks he does on a daily basis. We should, therefore, not be upset that he has benefited greatly from his ability to do something we cannot. It would be like us getting angry every time we see a bird fly. These inequalities and hierarchies are an entirely natural part of creation. They exist in virtually every society, in every species of animal, and without the direction of any Earthly force.

We all know from experience working in groups of more than five people or so, that a hierarchy always forms. Even without the imposed structure of a professional environment, a leader always emerges. There is invariably someone with raw talent or leadership abilities who takes command and gives orders. This is likely rooted in the power structure instituted by God where all power flows down from Him through His institutions both in Heaven and on Earth. As I noted earlier, Christianity embraces this inequality. Perhaps this is why FJC and conservatives are so comfortable with the inequalities in our society and in our government. They see it as part of a divinely established hierarchy which should be mimicked on Earth. It is the exemplary means of ordering society.

On the issue of gender, too, this can be applied. The inequalities between men and women—the difference in their natures—allows us to correctly order relationships between the genders. It sets roles for the sexes so that both can reach their full potential. This is not to say that women should be relegated to the kitchen—I do not think even FJC believes that—but that women should not be pushed by feminist ideologies to do something that is not right for them and will leave them unhappy or unfulfilled. In fact, the natural hierarchy might dictate that a woman becomes a doctor in translational medicine, while her husband never works a day in his life. In any case, an innate inequality is dictating the best outcomes for all involved.

Our republic as a whole, then, is not hindered by hierarchy but improved by it. According to FJC, it gains the advantageous development of an unfettered group of the nation's best and brightest—the natural aristocracy. These people, who have been educated and bred to know the spirit of the country and how best to serve it, keep the fickle and emotional populous in check.

These people are tasked with preserving the good of our republic. For, as FJC often says, a system of government—including a republic or a democracy—is not good by its own nature. It must be made good by what it produces. A democracy can result in just as much tyranny as a monarchy. The democratic mob rule of the French Revolution was bloodier than the reign of Louis XVI. Our system of government is only good because it guarantees our natural rights. When it stops doing that, it stops being good. This realization puts equality and the need for democracy on uneasy ground. A monarchy can be good if it protects our natural rights. The blatant inequality of a king is not a bad thing if he ensures that all of his subjects are free. We tend to get so hung up on the systems and methods of all we do that we forget that the end result is at least as important.[34]

Political and social equality can be great things if they are done right. If political equality means giving everyone the equal opportunity to achieve his fullest potential, FJC would argue, it results in prosperity for the nation and elevation for the soul of the individual. If social equality means not discriminating against people based on their race or gender and treating them with respect as individuals, then social equality is one of the most necessary aspects of our society. Once, however, the effort is made to create equal outcomes for individuals, tyranny will inevitably follow. Freedom cannot exist in an environment where government acts to abolish unequal outcomes. The United States, FJC argues, will not long survive after progressivism makes it impossible for one man to make himself unequal to another.

---

[34] Dear Uncle Screwtape reminds us, in C.S. Lewis' *The Screwtape Letters,* that "Democracy is the word with which you must lead them by the nose. The good work which our philological experts have already done in the corruption of human language makes it unnecessary to warn you that they should never be allowed to give this word a clear and definable meaning. They won't. It will never occur to them that *Democracy* is properly the name of a political system, even a system of voting, and that this has only the most remote and tenuous connection with what you are trying to sell them."

REPORT NO. 9:

LANGUAGE

Language is a fundamental part of what makes us human. Our ability to communicate and our means of communication defines who we are, both as individuals and as a species. The words we use carry immense value. They not only allow us to tell others what we think; they shape the way we think. For this reason, control of words means control of thought.

Humans think in language. The thoughts in our heads manifest themselves in the words we have heard and use in our everyday lives. An example of this comes from a TED Talk by Phuc Tran, a Vietnamese-born former professor of classics at Brooklyn College. Professor Tran discussed the role of the subjunctive mood in both English and Vietnamese. According to him, Vietnamese has no subjunctive mood, which means the language is limited in its ability to express conditional statements such as, "If there wasn't snow, then my flight wouldn't be canceled." The language tends to exclude possibilities in favor of naked reality. As a result, Tran explains, people like his father tend not to think in terms of what is possible. They tend to think in terms of what *is* rather than what *might have been*. This is a clear example of the language employed by the speaker having an effect on thoughts being formed. A person who does not think in terms of such possibilities does not concern himself terribly for the future. While it would be very beneficial to the progressive movement to alter the grammar of the English language to suppress thoughts of alternate futures, so changing the structure of the language would be almost impossible. We must, instead, settle for altering the words and phrases used by the American people to affect a similar change in thought processes.

The concrete things we see in the world around us are associated with the words we use. All aspects of the world we know are associated with the words we know. Studies of color recognition among different nationalities have found that Russians have an easier time than Americans at identifying different shades of the color blue because they have two different words which distinguish light blue from dark blue. Similarly, because we have the words red and pink, while Russians have a single word for red, красный (pronounced "*krassnee*"), English speakers have an easier time distinguishing shades of the color red than Russians. From this, it is evident that words even have the ability to influence what we see. The power to control a language, then, is one that can affect every part of a person's life.

From our social lives to our most deeply held beliefs, language is a great tool for giving shape to every form.

Why We Must Manipulate the Language

The great power of the English language presents the progressive movement with the opportunity to truly insert itself into the thoughts of the American people. But only if we make the appropriate alterations. There is no doubt, for those at the top of our movement, that English is in drastic need of reform. For one, it is not current. This is 2019, there are words and phrases that cannot be said anymore, yet still, often ring in our ears. In keeping with the dynamic progressive spirit, our language must be updated to keep with the times.

Staying modern with language is paramount for a movement that deals so directly with the country's popular social fashion. We cannot claim to be a movement that embraces the popular changes promoted by the American people if we do not use or encourage the use of the most modern phrases. More antiquated words that have fallen out of popular usage must also be abandoned in pursuit of modernity. Younger generations of Americans tend to have a relatively limited vocabulary on the whole. There are a lot of polysyllabic words—the sort popularized by William F. Buckley Jr.—with which they are not familiar. This, of course, is in part because of our effort to make school enjoyable for students instead of illuminating—a discussion for another time. The result is a slight disgust at these words among the youth. They feel that the user of such languages is either attempting to sound smarter than he actually is, or is the elitist sort who thinks speaking in big words makes him better than those around him. These are allegations that we should always try to levy against FJC and his college conservatives, but ones that we should be careful to avoid being turned on us. By removing words from the language that do not suit younger generations—and, in some cases, replacing them—we can become the only movement that makes an effort to speak the language of millennials.

The different groups of the American hierarchy that I described in the previous report can often be identified by their use of language. They use it as a means of belittling people and making clear their dominant role. The English language should be for everyone. It should be accessible to everyone. This will require us to dumb down the language for ease of understanding. It will require us to make unacceptable the kind of words that demonstrate a difference in class or knowledge. People should not be made to feel lesser because they are of lesser intelligence or because they have not benefited from the upbringing of the natural aristocracy. For progressivism to survive, language must be as egalitarian as it possibly can be. It should favor none and discourage none.

We can be the movement that appeals to those who believe that language is merely a tool to be used, not for pleasure or to be creative, but as a strict means of communicating simple ideas. In doing this, we can push the English language to better reflect the values for which we stand.

It is important that our language consists primarily of words and phrases that emphasize and color our progressive world view. In addition to removing words that are outdated and make people feel unequal, we will sneak into the list of deleted words those words that cause our movement a great deal of trouble. We will remove from acceptable language phrases that signal conservative ideology, such as "border security" and "law and order." Replacing it, instead, with something that conjures up images that dissuade people from supporting border security: phrases like "anti-immigrant policy" or "immediate deportation." The logic being that it will make it difficult for people to separate what we are telling them from reality. If the plan works, they will begin to view any policy intended to secure our borders as policy intended to take action against immigrants or the Mexican people. There will be no means of denoting intent or divorcing the policy from its negative effects. This method can be applied to numerous issues with similar effect.

Words that marginalized Americans find offensive, too, need to be eradicated from our vernacular. This goes back to our need to garner the support of the traditionally trodden upon. American blacks, gays, and the litany of other marginalized groups in this country will tend to lend their support to the organization that keeps them happy. If we can remove offensive language from these people's lives, then we can be confident we have their support, regardless of whether we actually help them. Look at America's black population as an example of this. We have, for the past thirty to forty years, been the movement that has consistently pushed for an alteration in language—among other things—to make black people happy. Despite the fact that the black population has seen very few appreciable gains as a result of progressive action, during that time period they continued to support us. They are still on the welfare we put them on in the 1960s, they still suffer from disproportionately poor education. They only seem to improve their situation during times of economic growth under Republican leadership, but they overwhelmingly vote for us because we sound less racist. Even I will admit that this is quite similar to people believing Donald Trump is unfit to be president because he does not act presidential. Just as Trump acts un-presidential, but accomplishes great things as president, so progressivism acts very racially sensitive, but does nothing to improve the plight of racial minorities. We rely on our words. We realize that language is so powerful, that just using it the right way can accomplish more for our movement than having to take actual actions. All we need to do is quell the insensitive jokes, admonish the stereotypes, and, generally, make people feel good about themselves, and we can accomplish great electoral success and garner huge popular support.

Making groups of Americans feel good also means adding in more inclusive language to our American vocabulary. This, first and foremost, means making English more gender-inclusive. For hundreds of years, the English-speaking world has been plagued by the grotesque use of "he" to describe an unnamed individual, who does not have an assigned gender, and who often does not actually exist. This use of "he" is, quite plainly, sexist. It degrades the value of the female. The English language needs to be altered to include "she" in these situations, or, for that matter, "zhe" to represent non-gender-specific persons. These additions are essential to begin rectifying the years of oppression caused by the vague use of "he," which has caused irreparable damage to generations of women. This linguistic inclusivity must, of course, extend to the use of words like "man" and "mankind" to represent the whole of humanity. While, for generations, it has been universally accepted among speakers of the English language that when the word "man" has been used, it refers to every member of the species, not just the male gender, it is important for those not so well-educated that the word "human" be used in its stead.[35] The word "human" indicates very clearly that it is not just the male gender being referenced. The same goes for "mankind" v. "humankind."

FJC would argue that the masculine has always been understood to represent the whole of the species and that attempts to change it now are made by feminists with "bugs up their asses" about the use of masculine words. This, he would argue, is likely the result of some pathological disdain for the male sex, nurtured by the traditional feminist stance that men are inherently guilty of oppressing women. FJC would continue that people who find a problem with the use of man to refer to all of humanity, should take issue with the majority of the world's languages before they take issue with English. In most languages, such as Spanish, it is a grammatical rule that groups of a mixed-sex must always be referred to using the masculine version of the noun. The fact that the majority of their nouns are only masculine or feminine—not any of the other genders—is problematic enough, but the constant preference for the masculine is more than a little concerning.

Words and phrases, then, must be used to placate this socially conscious group of people. The words that are supported and promulgated by our movement should mirror the social conscience of progressivism. This will ensure the enduring support of politically correct American society.

---

[35] In Old-English, the word *man* was exclusively non-gender-specific. A prefix of "wer" was required to make it specify the male sex, while the prefix "wif" was used to specify the female sex.

How to Manipulate the Language

Changing the American vernacular is something that is not actually terribly difficult to do. Most of the time, it happens without our intervention, but, unfortunately, also without our guidance. What we need to do, then, is guide the natural evolution of the English language in a way that accomplishes the goals noted above. This will allow us to hasten the transition to progressive language and prevent linguistic evolution from pulling in the wrong direction.

An easy technique for guiding the language in our direction is to associate the words that we are trying to remove from society with things that are disagreeable to young progressives and to the American people. The result of this will be to associate the people who say these words and phrases, (i.e., conservatives) with detestable ideas. A good example of this is one we have been pushing since the 1970s: the association of law and order with racism. It is no secret that conservative-minded individuals place the maintenance of law and order among their most sacred values. This makes it something that they will inevitably reference in their speeches and in their party platforms. When progressives associate law and order with racism, they are able to convince the general public that conservatives and the Republican Party are calling for racist policies when they propose an increase in law enforcement or even dare to ask for more respect for members of law enforcement.

This is just one example of ways we can alter language to create a negative perception of our ideological foes. All conservative language should be treated this way. Our movement must make a point of marking conservatives as hateful racists by continually responding to their words with accusations of bigotry. The result should, hopefully, be that every time a conservative opens his mouth, his words brand him a bigot. In this, we can go a very long way to discrediting all American conservatives by having them discredit themselves when they speak what they believe. We will have so changed the words they use into racially charged words of hate, that every one of their sentences will dig them deeper and deeper into racist slander.

This is where the progressive media becomes especially useful. It is the job of progressive media outlets to make public these racial slurs. It is their job to incriminate conservatives as the racists they are.

Through their "objective" reporting, anchors on these channels have the ability to shed light on instances where conservatives use the sort of language we have marked as racist. The job of the mainstream, progressive, media, then, is to check the language of conservative speakers and politicians every time they open their mouth and to subsequently levy accusations of racism against them.

The inbred effectiveness of using progressive media is a result of the longstanding trust of American people in these media outlets. Since the advent of television, NBC has consistently set the bar for reliable news coverage. It is the network of David Brinkley and Tom Brokaw, the objective standards of newscasting. When cable news first aired on American television screens, CNN was at the forefront. CNN very quickly became the go-to news source for most Americans. As a result of this history, these networks enjoy a level of prestige and national trust that is unquestioned.

The American people's faith in these networks means that they will believe virtually anything they say. When the networks toe the progressive line and inform the American public that the words used by conservatives indicate despicable intentions, the majority of people believe them. Why shouldn't they? These people have trusted these sources all their lives, so there is no reason to question them now.

The unquestioned belief in progressive news sources means that the progressive movement can have its way in the area of language. These networks authoritatively inform Americans when speech is both intellectually acceptable and in accord with their version of morality. Think about how many times you personally have heard a news outlet inform you that a politician is clearly out of touch with the majority of the American people because he has used a word that most people do not use on a regular basis. Think of how many times you yourself have judged a person arrogant because he used a big word. This is the result of the media telling the American people that it is elitist to do things that most people are unfamiliar with. That it is elitist to use the English language the way it was intended.

Along with the media's condemnation of words that set individuals apart from one another—words that make people unequal—they also tend to make moral assertions about the individual based on the words they use. This relates directly to the associations progressives make between conservative language and universally detested ideals. The media's role is cementing the notion that conservatives are inherently bad because of what they say. They do this also by cementing the alternative progressive language in the vernacular as the proper terminology.

A great example of this is in relation to illegal immigration. Not terribly long ago, when I was a child, I can clearly recall individuals who crossed into the United States from Mexico being referred to as "illegal aliens." This is still the most accurate legal term for the individuals to which I am referring, and it is one that makes clear the notion that they do not belong here. They are alien to our nation. In about a decade, the progressive media changed this term, slowly, so that it better reflected the way our movement wants to portray the people being described. By simply changing the words they said on television, over time, the progressive media changed the politically correct term from "illegal alien" to "illegal immigrant" to "undocumented immigrant." And all evidence points to the fact that, very soon, the majority of people, if they are not already, will be referring to individuals who have entered the United States illegally, simply as "immigrants," with nothing to distinguish them from the people who went through the pains of doing things properly. Most Americans will not notice the change. They will, though, feel its effects. They will have far more sympathy for the goals of the progressive movement as the language surrounding those goals changes.

While media cements these changes in the mainstream, icons of popular culture are, by far, the best at proliferating these changes primarily. These are the people that have the greatest influence in the lives of American youth. Younger Americans usually tend to embrace the language used in the popular culture. They use the words they hear in songs and in movies. They are impressed with this language and tend to make it their own. The progressive movement, which, more or less, owns the majority of America's popular icons, only needs these people to use the words we give them with some regularity. In doing this, we can use these stars to alter the vocabulary of all who are influenced by them. If we would like to change the politically correct term for black Americans, we can tell a black rapper to publically state that black Americans need to be referred to as _____. This will likely persuade a sizable portion of the American public—particularly white Americans who harbor some form of guilt for the sins of their long-deceased American forebears and who wish to always be on the cutting edge of political correctness.

While we use the institutions of American society at our disposal to spread the words we want to be used and to condemn those who use words we deem worthy of condemnation. We must also use progressives within our movement to ostracize people who use disagreeable language.

This effort to alienate those who use the wrong words—conservatives—must start at the university level. Progressive students must condemn their conservative peers as purveyors of hate speech whenever possible. They need to adopt the standards presented to them by popular culture and the media, using them to properly label other students at their respective universities.

Progressive students should ostracize their friends for using offensive language; they should organize protests against purveyors of conservative or alternative opinions, and they should use their small groups of very vocal activists to give the impression that the whole of the student body is enraged by conservative language. They should do as students at St. Augustine University of Philadelphia did when the College Republicans, under FJC's predecessor, invited Milo Yiannopoulos to speak on campus. Progressive students must protest freedom of speech, condemn the speaker, and demand that the university in question prohibit the speaker from going through with the engagement. In doing these things, progressive students will both make life more difficult for their conservative peers—hopefully dissuading them from future activities—and also eliminate threats to on-campus progressive hegemony.

Individual progressive actions will not work in the long run if they are limited to happening only on college campuses. Students are only there for four years. The consequences of embracing conservative language need to be felt long after the conservative matriculates through school. It must be felt in the job market. Progressive employers must look at all the social engagements of their prospective hires to ensure that, at no point, they used any phrases that have been deemed politically incorrect. If the progressive employer does see these phrases in articles the potential employee has written or on that person's social media, they must refuse to offer the applicant job placement. Employees must ensure that the conservative feels pain for choosing to be who he is. The methods used to change the language will all be justified in their brutality and heavy-handedness. This is an important battle for the progressive movement to win. Success here means potential for progressives to reshape the American way of thinking entirely. It means dictating the images in the heads of millions of Americans. It means capturing the minds and imaginations of the nation. Language is so much of humanity that proper manipulation of it means unprecedented control for progressivism. With the right amount of control over the language, progressivism can make the ideology of the Left the sole ideology in the United States.

Effects of Manipulating the Language

FJC will undoubtedly respond to our plan by accusing us of, among other things, destroying the English language. He, for some reason, cares a great deal for this tool of American communication. He and people like him, who place a value on words and their usage for their own sake, will see what we are doing as an affront to that which is beautiful. They will see our attempts to strip English of its elitism as our destroying its beauty. Rather like chopping down a forest to make a public park or building a hydro-electric power station on a babbling brook.

While it is true that we may, in fact, be making the language less descriptive and, for those interested in something other than practical usage, more dreary, we will also be making it more inclusive. By limiting it, we will be expanding the number of people who can access it. Instead of forcing people to expand their vocabulary and learn new phrases, we will be bringing the language down to their level. We believe doing this will make Americans more equal and America friendlier to the disadvantaged.

Our constant policing of language, through progressive media and popular culture, as well as the accusations of hatred and bigotry that will accompany that policing, should result in the American people policing themselves. Americans will live in constant fear of being accused of racism and bigotry as a result of their words. Every time a person speaks publicly, he will increasingly fear that, at the end of his speech, he will walk away a bigot. This will cause them to be extremely careful with their words and to refrain from saying exactly what they mean. Conservatives will suffer immensely as a result of this. Because we have labeled conservative language as bigoted, most conservatives will never open their mouths. This is already the case on college campuses. Even at the relatively conservative St. Augustine University of Philadelphia, we see that conservative opinion is only actually vocalized by a few members of College Republicans, led by FJC. The great personal pains he has had to go through to coax conservative students into speaking their minds is one of the minor victories of our movement. College students who value their social standing and value the grades they receive from progressive-minded professors suppress themselves for fear of being ostracized by their peers and of being graded poorly by their instructors.

Eventually, the whole of the conservative world will live in the kind of fear that conservative students now experience. Eventually, through public humiliation and occupational repercussions, more and more adult conservatives will begin to suppress themselves. When enough conservatives stop speaking, only progressive voices will be heard. Only progressive language will then exist.

When all communication is accomplished using words approved by the progressive movement, and when we are rid of phrases that communicate conservative ideals, the American people will be unable to produce non-progressive thoughts. They will have great difficulty comprehending anything outside of the language that we will be giving them. Our culture is defined by our language. A progressive language means a progressive culture means a progressive people.

APPENDIX A

The Conservatives on Campus: St. Augustine College Republicans

As Published in *The Hippo*

When the first issue of National Review was published, its founder William F. Buckley Jr. wrote, "it stands athwart history yelling Stop, at a time when no one is inclined to do so or have much patience with those who so urge it." Today, on college campuses across the nation, very little patience is shown for conservative students who are accused of standing athwart the social justice movement and the prevailing liberal political culture. These conservative students—these "non-licensed non-conformists"—need a platform to express and discuss their principles. The College Republicans of St. Augustine University of Philadelphia is that platform.

St. Augustine College Republicans will create an environment at St. Augustine where conservative students can feel free to express their opinions freely and vigorously without fear of intimidation. To this end, we as an organization will speak loudly in defense of our liberties, our capitalist system, our American way of life, our Judeo-Christian values, our Republican candidates, our Constitution, and our president. We will show the quiet conservatives at St. Augustine that many—if not most—of their classmates agree with them. We will foster the growth of a campus where conservatives do not feel outnumbered or fear being ostracized.

St. Augustine College Republicans see it as our responsibility to defend and advance the freedoms that we Americans hold dear. Our organization will work tirelessly to expand what Thomas Jefferson called the "Empire of Liberty" within the hearts and minds of St. Augustine students. It will be our goal to provide Augustinians with speakers and events which remind them why the United States is the greatest country on Earth. At a time when many on the Left proclaim our nation a land of racists and homophobes, it is more important than ever that students see the United States for what it truly is, "a nation conceived in liberty" and "the last best hope for man on Earth."

As a conservative organization at an Augustinian university, one of our primary goals must be pushing back against the pervasive trend of moral relativism. We will do our part to ensure that Augustinians graduate knowing that in this world there is such thing as right and wrong and that these concepts are absolute. Altering morality is not acceptable just because the world is different now from what it was 200 years ago. The social fashion of the moment must never be allowed to dictate morality. St. Augustine is an Catholic university and so our values and morals are rooted in the core dogmas of the Church and in the word of God, making them eternal and absolute.

Lastly, our organization will work to foster unity and dialogue both as Augustinians and as Americans. We will actively combat the divisive scourge of identity politics that pits racial, religious, ethnic, gender, and social groups against one another, making us less of a nation. We will foster diversity where it actually matters, in ideas. It is our firm belief that an individual is defined by his character and ideals, not by race or ethnicity.

We believe our club will succeed in accomplishing its goals and doing what is Right. It must succeed.

The College Republicans of St. Augustine University welcomes students of principle to help us accomplish our goals and do their part in preserving the nation we love.

Executive Board
College Republicans
St. Augustine University of Philadelphia

APPENDIX B

I Vow to Thee My Country
Lyrics by Cecil Spring-Rice
Music by Gustav Holst

I vow to thee, my country, all earthly things above,
entire and whole and perfect, the service of my love:
the love that asks no question, the love that stands the test,
that lays upon the altar the dearest and the best;
the love that never falters, the love that pays the price,
the love that makes undaunted the final sacrifice.

And there's another country I've heard of long ago,
most dear to them that love her, most great to them
that know;
we may not count her armies, we may not see her King;
her fortress is a faithful heart, her pride is suffering;
and soul by soul and silently her shining bounds increase,
and her ways are ways of gentle-
ness and all her paths are peace.[36]

---

[36] "I Vow to Thee, My Country, All Earthly Things Above." Hymnary.org. Accessed October 7, 2018. https://hymnary.org/text/i_vow_to_thee_my_country.

ABOUT THE AUTHOR

 Frank J. Connor is a graduate of Villanova University class of 2019 where he studied economics and served as president of Villanova University College Republicans spreading the conservative message on campus. In the summer of 2016, Frank worked in Congressman Scott Garrett's office handling constituents' concerns and learning what the American people expect of their government. That same summer, he began his writing career with Western Free Press, publishing articles of conservative opinion. In 2017, Frank was appointed to the Bergen County Republican Committee in his home state of New Jersey, making him its youngest member. Frank now works to prepare younger generations of conservatives for the intellectual battles they will face in college and the years following.